ALIEN "MOST WANTED"

Veteran NYPD Lieutenant Patrick Brogan drew a wild card in the intergalactic Law Enforcement Exchange program.

Brogan and his partner Jack Haldane have been assigned to the toughest precinct in the galaxy—Demeter City on the planet Altor, a crime-ridden intergalactic crossroads where alien perps and otherworldly outlaws battle the law and batter one another in a melting pot of mayhem and murder.

Here, where every scam and hustle in the known universe is played out by the galaxy's Most Wanted, Brogan and Haldane are writing a whole new rulebook for law enforcement.

Space Precinct

Where the perps and the problems are truly out of this world!

Gerry Anderson's
SPACE PRECINCT

The Deity-Father
Demon Wing
Alien Island

From HarperPrism

Gerry Anderson's

SPACE PRECINCT

◆ ALIEN ISLAND ◆

DAVID BISCHOFF

HarperPrism
An Imprint of HarperPaperbacks

HarperPaperbacks   *A Division of* HarperCollins*Publishers*
10 East 53rd Street, New York, N.Y. 10022

Copyright © 1996 by Grove Television Enterprises
All rights reserved. No part of this book may be used or reproduced in any manner whatsoever without written permission of the publisher, except in the case of brief quotations embodied in critical articles and reviews. For information address HarperCollins*Publishers*, 10 East 53rd Street, New York, NY 10022.

Cover illustration © 1996 by Grove Television Enterprises

First printing: February 1996

Printed in the United States of America

HarperPrism is an imprint of HarperPaperbacks. HarperPaperbacks, HarperPrism, and colophon are trademarks of HarperCollins*Publishers*.

❖ 10 9 8 7 6 5 4 3 2 1

To Gerry Anderson . . .
and Gene Roddenberry, Rod Serling,
J. Michael Straczynski, Joseph Stefano,
and the others who've brought science fiction
series to television.

Acknowledgments

Thanks to Caitlin Deinard Blasdell,
John Silbersack, Chris Schelling,
Sara Schwager, and Jimmy Vines
for all the hard work behind the scenes.

SPACE PRECINCT

◆ ALIEN ISLAND ◆

PROLOGUE

This is the Alien Island.

Not a Xenotropic Isthmus, nor a Strange Archipelago.

The Alien Island.

Twenty kilometers by ten, it sits like a punctuation dot below the southern hemisphere of the continent on the planet Altor, which contains Demeter City.

A riot of life, its layers of jungle are among the densest in the universe, and yet Dreek—for that is its name in the local lingo—is a place of many biomes, many levels, plains as well as a pimpling of hills. This is why it is such an astonishing and useful place for the purposes of those civilized beings who use it.

The civilized being of the moment is neither in hills nor plains now.

He is in the jungle.

This is the hunter.

Call him Maelish.

Maelish was a Creon by persuasion and habit, and it was not often that his hardworking life allowed him the luxury of spending time gripping a big-bore gun, sweating profusely, and experiencing the joy and thrill of the Hunt. Creons by ancestry were, like humans, hunter-gatherers originally. It was only in the latter part of their development that they'd tilled the soil and built up their bogs and generally done the agricultural thing. Hunting, then, was an instinct just beneath their veneer of civilization.

So now, as he strode cautiously through the jungles of Dreek Island, Maelish felt his blood rising. His nostrils quivered in their search for prey, and his ears twitched. His big eyes twirled about in their majestically stereoscopic excellence. It was this feature of the Creon physiology that gave them such excellent vision: big twenty-twenty eyes, spread *wide* apart. Now, although all of his other senses were finely tuned, Maelish could see through the fronds and vines and *bugga* trees before him with incredible depth perception and clarity.

So far, however, those excellent eyes saw no *zark*.

Maelish stopped for a moment, allowing his heavy *visht* gun to rest in one arm as he pulled out a cloth and mopped his considerable brow. He took a swig of water from his canteen and then squinted up at the sun, just coming down from its zenith and westering in the thick-leafed branches of the upper canopy of the forest.

He had hunted for two hours, with no sign or spoor from the beast. But he knew it was out there. Not just because he was a hunter, though. It was also because he was a cop. He'd hunted his share of criminals through the jagged byways of Demeter City on this planet Altor, and although he was far from being a Tarn, he could nevertheless *sense* that the *zark* was out there just as he could sense criminals around the corner, without even being able to see them. The great thing about the jungle, about this scenario, though, was that you could focus. You didn't have to worry about traffic and passersby and onlookers getting in the way. You just went for your quarry and nabbed it.

Maelish felt focused now; only he was getting a bit tired, a bit drained. He longed for the excitement of confrontation! The sighting of the brave beast! Perhaps a snarl, a roar, a charge!

And then he would line up his crosshairs . . . Steady . . . steady there . . .

Boom!

Yowl! Bestial flesh exploding. The mighty creature hitting the dust. Another trophy for Maelish, brave hunter!

Something rustled in the bushes.

Maelish's senses alerted him immediately. He swung his gun around in the general direction of the disturbance.

Insects chirred. A vine swayed. The damp mask

of humidity hovered over everything, a sweat ghost.

Maelish swiveled his gun from point to point. Had that sound just been his imagination?

No, of course not. All his inner alarms were going off like crazy.

Something was out there.

He smiled grimly to himself. Well, at least he wasn't bored anymore!

The distinctive sound seemed to have come from over there, to the northeast, by that copse of *sancha* trees. Maelish knew the names of his flora and fauna all right. It was all part of the whole thing, living his role, being one not only with Nature but with consciousness's view of Nature. Names and labels had purposes. They helped you to navigate. Intelligence was handy. It helped you build big guns, like the one he carried now.

He was just entering a clearing, the sweet-sour smell of *clarka* flowers in his nostrils, when he heard it.

A voice!

"Maelish! Yo! Maelish!"

He spun.

"Up here, my friend!"

Maelish looked up.

In the crook of a tree, holding a hunting rifle similar to his, was another Creon. He was slightly smaller than Maelish, definitely a smaller head— but with a sleeker, better-muscled body, broad shoulders, powerful thighs.

"Cradla! Hello!" said Maelish. "Out hunting *zark*

as well, perhaps. I thought, though, that I'd requested this area all to myself."

"Out hunting, but not necessarily *zark*, good fellow lawkeeper. May I join you? I promise . . . Any *zark* out here is all yours!"

Maelish considered. This was unusual, but not beyond possibility. Particularly considering Cradla's position here on the island—and on the force. He'd always gotten along with the guy himself, but never had been exactly buddy-buddy. Now that Maelish seemed headed up the ladder, though, was there any question about why Cradla would like to be better friends? No, of course not! Cradla saw him now as a peer, and naturally would consider a close association to be mutually beneficial.

"Of course, my friend. It would be an honor! Besides, you know these jungles far better than I do, with your experience of the island and your position on the Shadda Lattice. Perhaps you might give me a few tips."

"Tips? Of course, I'd be happy to give you as many tips as you like!" Smiling, Cradla jumped smoothly and easily from his perch, taking the two-plus-meter fall with feline grace. He rose easily from his springed haunches and showed bright teeth in a grin to his colleague. "First off, I suppose you'd very much like to know where the *zark* might be hiding?"

"I didn't know that *zarks* hid."

"A figure of speech. As a matter of fact, on my walk just a few minutes ago, I thought I caught a glimpse of its tail"—Cradla pointed northwest—"just over there."

"Oh excellent. The jungle seems a bit less dense."

"Shall we, then?"

"Yes. Thank you, Cradla."

They fell into step abreast, Maelish complimenting his colleague by holding his weapon in exactly the same way.

"Ah," said Cradla, "is it not invigorating to return to our savage roots?"

"Oh yes. I feel my blood roar! I feel my brothers close to me. I feel more alive than ever when I am out on the hunt. . . . Indeed, feeling my savage roots, as you say!"

"Only feeling slightly more confident, propped with modern weaponry!" suggested Cradla, slyly.

Maelish was taken aback.

As his grass-stained boots clopped through the dirt and undergrowth, he wondered what was the best response to this kind of statement. Maelish decided finally to assume that his colleague was jesting.

"And *excellent* weaponry. Good equipment is always important to properly masculine Creons!"

Cradla laughed, and patted his traveling companion on the back. "Indeed! The gun makes the Creon!"

"Walk softly, but carry a big gun!"

The two chuckled together as they walked farther into dense jungle, and Maelish was gratified to feel the good sensations of male Creon bonding fill him.

"It cannot be long before we find your quarry," said Cradla. "And I shall rejoice in your victory.

Tell me—in whose names will you dedicate your kill this evening to the Gathering!"

"Well, naturally, because of your aid . . . I will include you . . . "

"Oh. A pleasant surprise!"

"And of course I shall have to include Captain Podly of Demeter Precinct 88, to whom I owe much for my recent ascent to the position I now enjoy."

"Ah. Podly. Yes. You are close friends with Podly, yes?"

"Friends? Podly?" Maelish laughed, and this time his laughter was real and not forced. "Hardly. He does not care much for me, I think. However, he feels my service and capabilities to be excellent, and therefore felt I deserved the increase in responsibilities"—sweat dripped into the Creon's smile—"and the added fraternity of the island!"

"Podly," said Cradla, nodding to himself. "Yes, Podly is a crusty one, is he not? Some would say that if not for him, then I would be captain of the precinct!"

"Oh? I had not heard such—"

Maelish halted himself immediately, realizing that he might be offending his companion. However, he was happy to see that Cradla's face remained pleasant and unprovoked.

"But of course, what do I know?"

"Indeed," said Cradla. "You are merely a newcomer. How could you be expected to know about the intrigues and politics that have stirred the Brotherhood for years and years. However, ultimately, we must remember . . . that our fraternity is what matters, no? We must resolve any differences, and place all due emphasis on solidarity in the matter at hand."

"Yes, of course! To complete the course at hand," recited Maelish. "To keep the peace! To defend the law-abiding, and to bring all scofflaws and criminals to justice!"

"Doubtless you can recite all of the Brotherhood's Creed from stem to stern, hmm?"

"Oh, indeed. Would you like to hear me?"

"I am too impressed now, Brother. Such would overwhelm me!"

Again, Maelish didn't know which way to take Cradla's phrasing and, therefore, because it had a slight sting of sarcasm to it, he decided that the Creon was joking.

"Oh, I am *more* impressed by your capabilities, I'm sure."

"Well you should be, Brother. Thank you, though, for your thoughts."

Maelish didn't know how to take that last phrase, but he didn't have much time to consider how he should respond because ahead, blasting through the forest, came a guttural and ferocious growl.

"The *zark*!"

"None other! Did I not tell you it was in this direction? But look for yourself. Over there, just past that clearing!"

Maelish stepped forward, craning his neck, even as he brought his weapon up and placed his hand on the trigger. "I hear it, but I certainly don't see it."

"What's wrong with your eyes? There, just behind that tree!" said Cradla.

Maelish took another two long steps in the direction that his companion pointed. The tree that Cradla referred to was a *gosha* tree, with a very thick bole. So perhaps another step . . .

And there it was.

Despite himself, Maelish gasped.

The creature had six legs, all of them clawed, and looked to weigh about three or four times Maelish's own considerable weight. There wasn't much on the head except for fangs and barbs. The eyes were tiny slices of hellfire, and they most certainly saw the Creons approaching. . . .

And didn't care for the sight much.

"It's a big one!" said Maelish.

"You've shot *zarks* before. . . ?"

"I've shot plenty of large game animals before." Which wasn't quite the truth.

"But *zarks*?"

"Well, smaller ones."

In VirtReal simulations! In actuality, he'd shot game animals in real life, yes . . .

But never anything so terrifying as this!

"Same principle. Aim, fire, kill."

Maelish nodded. Somehow, he managed to fight down his panic, pull up his gun.

The *zark* was wasting no time.

Somehow, it managed to accelerate from zero to fast in virtual nanoseconds.

Maelish found the beast in his crosshairs. *Steady there, fellow*, he told himself. *You're probably going to get one shot, and that is it.*

The sound of gunfire.

His legs went out from under him, and a numbness spread over his body. His vision went in and out in winks, and he saw things in flashes.

The *zark*, still coming, fast.

The blast of another round of fire.

The *zark* tumbling, a bloody mass.

Then, Cradla, coming around to face him, gun smoking.

Grinning.

"You wouldn't have hit the thing, bumbler. I took care of that. Just as I'm taking care of you."

He aimed the gun at Maelish.

The Creon croaked a sound that managed to sound like: "Why?"

"Maybe because Podly likes you better," said Cradla. "And maybe because you're in my way. Oh . . . and don't worry . . . Captain Podly will be joining you very soon."

Thus, with a *coup de grace*, did Maelish's hunting trip come to an explosive and preemptive end.

CHAPTER

Precinct 88 of the Demeter Police hovers many kilometers above Demeter City of the planet Altor in precise geosynchronous orbit. Here it is as out-of-reach for most of that infamous city's criminal element as its nearby orbiting sister, the Space Suburb, where many of its officers live.

Precinct 88 often thundered with the commanding tones of its chief officer, bent on the task of making Demeter City a safer, better place.

Today, however, that voice was softer and more considerate:

Gentle beings," said Captain Podly, "I think it's time."

Lieutenant Patrick Brogan paused in mid-sip of his brackish precinct coffee and looked over at his boss, sitting back in his chair at his position of command: his desk. "Time for what, sir?"

"Yeah!" said Officer Jack Haldane, examining his wrist chronometer. "We just got here. You gonna let us go home early, Captain? That would be great! I've got a project under way that I wouldn't mind working on."

A bushy eyebrow above a commanding eye rose. "No. Nothing like less work—today, in any case." He leaned his big body, encased in Demeter Police blues, forward, his huge Creon head tilting precariously above it. His big lids did a wipe of big eyes and the bright pupils looked out of them.

Not, however, with their usual grumpiness, but with actual benevolence.

"No, I have something special in mind for you two. Something I think you're going to like."

Brogan was taken aback.

From the moment he'd arrived to help keep the law enforcement engine ticking on Demeter City, he'd never known Captain Podly *ever* to precede any kind of announcement with "You're going to *like* this!" Quite the opposite, in fact. Generally it was more a gruff "Guys, you're going to *hate* this assignment." Morosely and with great satisfaction.

All in all it made Brogan nervous.

"Captain Podly, you've become so thoroughly acquainted with human psychology that you know what Jack and I are going to like," said Brogan doubtfully.

"Season tickets to the Galactic Baseball Series! That's what I'd like!" said Jack.

"I think you'll like this better, Jack." Podly wrapped his hands around the back of his head in a gesture that seemed positively *smug*. "And as for human psychology . . . well, there are sufficient similarities. Particularly in human and Creon *male* psychologies. Yes, I think that this announcement definitely will appeal."

"Gee, Captain, you're going to make us die with suspense," said Haldane. "Out with it!"

Brogan knew Haldane felt comfortable demanding this, albeit in a jocular fashion. Podly generally kept everyone at a distance—he was a crusty kind of guy—but at more casual times like these he permitted rough jokes and backslapping male-type stuff. Podly was a man's alien—no question about it.

"Yeah, Captain, dammit. We could use some good news!" Brogan added his two credits' worth of abrasion.

Those big, limpid eyes twinkled. He leaned his smile forward. "I'm takin' you guys to Dreek Island!"

Brogan blinked.

Haldane looked over to Brogan, a clear "Huh?" in his expression.

"Are we supposed to know what Dreek Island is?" asked Brogan.

"Are we supposed to *care* what Dreek Island is? That's the question," said Haldane.

Disappointment showed on Captain Podly's face. "What? I thought you knew."

"You've never mentioned it before," said Brogan.

"Surely . . . I mean . . . I just supposed that you'd heard the term bandied about in the locker room." He shook his head. "Orrin never mentioned it?"

"Nope," said Haldane.

"Not a word," said Brogan.

Podly harrumphed. He eyed them both in a manner that could have been quizzing, could have been doubtful, and then cleared his throat. He rose up, put his hands behind his back, and began to pace the area behind his desk like a constipated John Wayne after a long horse ride.

"Dreek Island symbolizes a great deal to the lawkeeping of this great police force. It is a place where Demeter City's finest can . . . well, let us say, discover each other—and themselves."

Haldane nodded thoughtfully. "Some kind of social club?"

"Sounds more like a fraternity," said Brogan. "Sure, we've got that back on Earth, Captain. Why on an island, though?"

"Fraternity?" Podly went to a wall, where he studied a display of his various multitude of awards, certificates, and honors. Multicolored ribbons and strands of some equally vibrant material seemed to be in favor within the alien police force. "Ah, yes . . . a brotherhood! Of sorts, I suppose." He fingered an arrangement of shell-like things, formed to resemble his head. He inadvertently pressed a button, and motorized eyeballs twirled in the eye sockets. A purple tongue lolled. Some kind of gag gift, it would seem. In an embarrassed flurry, Podly hastily thumbed it off. "Yes—right. Dreek Island. You must excuse me. In my enthusiasm for the subject, I've quite skipped the name of our organization."

"Organization name," said Haldane. "Now you're way past us for sure. Brogan, you heard of any organization names around here?"

"Not offhand."

"Nope," announced Haldane with finality. "None."

"We're called the GOKS. The Gathering of Kindred Souls," Podly announced proudly. "The organization predates the Demeter Police system. It started on Danae, the Creon home planet. When we allied with the Tarns, on this planet, the males of that race proved themselves worthy of the ranks of the GOKS . . . speedily, I might add. There have been the occasional problems with the Tarns, but never lack of respect. . . . Yes . . . well, let us simply say that Dreek Island is more or less the headquarters of our society. It is where we gather for recreation and ritual. . . . It was a fortunate find. The primary ritual being, of course, initiation."

That strange phenomenon known as a Creon smile revealed thick sturdy Creon teeth.

Brogan got it.

"Captain. You mean . . ."

The light had dawned in Haldane's brain as well. "You're asking us to join your organization?"

"Yes. You'll be the first humans." Podly's head nodded slightly with uncharacteristic enthusiasm. "The first human males. We don't allow females, you see."

Patrick Brogan got a little thrill of excitement. This wasn't exactly a milestone in intergalactic relationships, but it was important to him. Podly doing the thing that best expressed, to him and his fellows, how much value they now placed on their colleagues from Earth. It was more than friendship. It was . . . It was . . .

"A men's club!" said Haldane, looking as pleased as Brogan felt. "Captain Podly, that's *great*." He put out a hand. "Thanks so much!"

Handshaking Earth-style was something Podly had taken to immediately, and it was clear he was putting his heart into it as he pumped Haldane's hand. The police captain turned to Brogan, and the handsome, fortyish, blond man accepted the huge appendage with enthusiasm. However, even as Podly exerted manly pressure, and Haldane looked as though he was about to slap them both on their backs, Brogan had a troubling thought.

"Uhm. What about the women?"

"Women?" said Podly.

"Sorry. Females."

"What about them?"

A funny look passed over Haldane's face. The kind of look a blissful partier might get upon observing a large amount of fecal matter abruptly dropped into a punch bowl.

"Well, this isn't the dark ages of the twentieth century, after all. . . ."

Man had reached the stars, and Woman . . . well, women were right along with them. . . .

Just as promised on that old TV show, mankind had gone Where No One Had Gone Before . . . Almost.

The Universe was densely populated with many different races, with unimaginably diverse variations on the theme of biology and intelligence . . . and many odd parallels to Earth.

Nor was it exactly by their own power that Mankind had reached those stars.

What had happened was this.

Earth had been contacted.

There were many reasons why the governing intelligences of the Universe had contacted the UN and the governments it represented, less than ten years before. A desire for a meeting of minds, a natural curiosity, an open policy which welcomed new and upcoming civilizations in the galaxy . . .

However, it also became readily apparent that there was something that galactic civilizations admired very much about Earth.

Their lawkeeping systems.

Most specifically, the NYPD.

The New York Police Department.

Brogan and Haldane were New York cops. A couple of the very best. That was why they were here now, on Demeter City, on the planet called Altor, the hub of galactic civilization. Demeter City had a bit of everything in the Known Universe . . . And a large part of the crime.

There was a kind of Talent, as well as an Informational, Exchange between planets, and it was thus that Patrick Brogan found himself with an amazing opportunity. Live on an alien planet— and still stay a cop! His wife and kids jumped at the opportunity, and now they resided, for safety reasons, on a space suburb in synchronous orbit with Altor. However, they got down to Demeter City regularly, taking part in the activities and mixing with the various life-forms there.

Nor were they the only ones . . .

Plenty of humans had come to Demeter City.

However, it would appear that only two *male* humans would be going to Dreek Island to be initiated into a special club.

This would not sit well with certain other members of this Space Precinct; nor would his dear liberated wife Sally like it much.

Brogan said as much to Podly.

He was rewarded with incomprehension.

"But . . . But . . ." said the Creon. "They are *female*. How can they belong to a club of all males?"

"Creon and Tarn women accept this 'male' tradition?" asked Brogan.

"Of course!"

Haldane sighed, scratching his youthful dark hair. "I suppose we'd have to go into all kinds of sociopolitical Earth history to explain it to him. Is it really worth it?"

"No. Maybe not."

This was too important an opportunity to bond with an alien race in ways important to it to pay attention to Politically Correct Policy.

Maybe, for the time being, with Podly's help, they could just conceal that unfortunate aspect of this whole matter and not point out to any females that it was a purely male affair . . .

Maybe.

He suggested this to Podly.

Podly shrugged. "If that makes you feel better." The smile returned. "You'll accept my invitation. You'll join us. You'll both come to Dreek Island?"

Brogan opened his mouth to accept.

Another voice chimed from behind them.

"A Greek island? My, my, it sounds exotic and exciting."

A female voice. Brogan spun around and found Jane Castle leaning toward them quizzically, thumbs in pockets in her Rosalind Russell Gal Friday pose.

"Jane!" said Haldane.

"Hello, Castle," said Brogan, looking a bit sheepish despite himself.

"Officer Castle," gruffed Podly. "I do not believe I summoned you to my office."

"Privacy shield's not down. Sorry, sir," said the young woman, losing her casual manner immediately with the touch of Podly's domineering mode. She pulled out a piece of paper that had been folded up under her arm and politely placed it on the lip of the police captain's desk. "That report you requested, sir."

Brogan wondered guiltily if she'd heard any of the previous conversation. She was a spunky kid, Jane Castle, and she'd fought hard to get where she was. One word of male chauvinism generally set her off on a diatribe. The concept of an exclusive *male* club of police officers would not be to her liking at all, and no wonder. Brogan, dyed-in-the-wool New York cop that he was, steeped in all that manly Irish tradition, knew that women police officers worked just as hard as their male counterparts—hell, harder even—and deserved just as much inclusion and respect. He was embarrassed because he knew that there was no way he was going to blow this chance of getting closer to his alien colleagues by demanding that Jane or others be included in this honor.

Officer Jane Castle was a slender, attractive, European cop who'd been on Demeter when Brogan arrived. She'd helped him learn the ropes. She was the kind of young woman a guy could get attached to. Brogan was quite fond of her. Jack Haldane had a huge crush on her that he didn't even try to hide. Castle, though, seemed impervious to all but his nonsexual charms. She was auburn-haired with bright eyes and a chipper, alive attitude toward the world, engaging everything with zeal and compassion. As far as Brogan was concerned, she was the second most sexy, beautiful, and intelligent woman this side of Alpha Centauri. Number one, of course, being his wife, Sally.

That, and she always smelled nice, too. Her rosy glow was a nice refreshing touch to this area, dominated by Podly's Creon musk-grouch miasma.

"Officer Castle," said Podly. "Are you aware of the sophisticated computer system this precinct station owns?"

"Of course, sir, I just thought—"

"Thinking doesn't always become you, Officer Castle," said Podly, clearly miffed that the flow of this special moment had been interrupted. He grabbed up the paper in his big paw, examined it. "Heavens name. What's this?" He batted the paper.

Brogan lifted himself on his toes and peered. On the paper, by the printout, was a drawing of what appeared to be a Creon head.

"I just thought I'd try an artist's rendering of the description of the suspect. Expand myself."

Podly's mottled lips quivered. "This is the worst drawing of a Creon I've ever seen in my life!"

"Looks like a pretty good Creon to me!" said Haldane, smiling solicitously at Castle, who did not acknowledge the compliment.

"Good! *Good?*" thundered Podly. "Where's the nobility of the Creon brow! The individuality of each Creon eye and orb? The proud chin, the amazing ears . . . the beauty and grace that is each Creon's Rax-Deity–bestowed birthright? Why—this looks like a human being wearing an atrocious mask and makeup."

"Sorry, sir," said Castle. Her apology did not seem particularly heartfelt to Brogan.

"Perhaps in the future you should confine your artistic doodlings to your own species," said Podly, scratching at the whiskered, pimplelike bumps below his chin. "As for what we've been talking about—I'm afraid it's absolutely none of your business."

"No Greek Island, I'm afraid. Business," murmured Brogan, almost apologetically.

"Hey, you know, if you want a Greek Island," said Haldane, "I'll put in a call to my friend Zeus. Zeus Kakastontites, Bargain Travel Agency, back on Earth. He can get us a nice cruise!"

Castle rolled her eyes in her usual "Will this Dud-stud ever stop trying?" manner, muttered another apology, and stomped away.

"Isn't she cute when she's flummoxed?" said Haldane.

"Females!" said Podly. "I'm afraid our species suffer alike in that department." He shook his ungainly head. "Can't breed without them, can't make *nasham* cakes with them."

Brogan was about to offer a similar, more-to-the-point, Earthly homily, but thought better of it. The thought was intended to be affiliating, but it might sound like one-upmanship.

"Yeah," said Haldane. "Females. Can't live with them, can't live without them!"

Podly canted his head. "Excellent. An Earth saying?"

"You bet," affirmed Haldane. "Number one on the male hit parade at fraternities and Freemason lodges everywhere."

Light gleamed at the back of Podly's eyes. "I *like* it. You must stand up and give that saying to all at the GOKS upon Dreek Island.

Haldane grinned smugly at Brogan. Brogan felt like beaning him. Oh well. Brogan had his own share of sayings. Right in his *Bartlett's Quotations*. He'd just have to do a little brushing up. Also, maybe a few jokes. Those always went down well on fishing trips in the Adirondacks with the guys back home.

"Gentle beings, I cannot hide the fact that I am pleased. Very pleased," said Podly. He stamped the flat of his left hand over his heart—well, to his right lower abdomen. "This is a proud organization of lawkeepers here on Demeter City. And the GOKS are the *warg* cream. I have the feeling that you two will add to the fat content of that *warg* cream, to say nothing of good old-fashioned stench-filled brave sweat."

"Remind me not to order a sundae on this island," said Haldane out of the side of his mouth to his partner.

Podly frowned. "What was that?"

"I said it sounds like a GOKS week on this island will be like a month of Sundays!" said Haldane, louder.

Podly still looked confused, but he let it pass. "Now, on to more deadly business." He leaned over, giving them his Grade A serious-as-cancer gaze. "Lieutenant Brogan, Officer Haldane, it has come to my attention that we may have an extremely dangerous assassin at work in our fair city!"

CHAPTER

Killing Tarns was not a particularly easy task, what with their telekinetic and psychic powers and all. You get *too* close to the bastards, they could smell you. They could sense your dark intentions and they got defensive, which made them very difficult marks.

That was why he had a .456 carbine Sharpshooter Rifle.

Old-fashioned, but effective. Sniper time. What was good for John F. Kennedy in the twentieth century would be quite effective now. Nice thing about hits—be they human or alien, you tear out enough brain, heart matter, or viscera, your job is done.

He sat atop a building, under an awning, smoking a cigarette and having himself some iced *maka* tea. The day was typical Demeter City smoggy grey as the sun struggled to make it through the gunk that the many unfettered factories spewed into the atmosphere. The skyline was filled with traffic and the skywalks crowded with pedestrians, but he had chosen a good spot. Up here he was well-nigh unnoticeable.

He checked his augmented binoculars, then his watch. Another few moments until kill time. He used the opportunity to meditate, reflect, and generally prepare himself for the task ahead. He'd perforated plenty of people on Earth, but not too many on Demeter City, and those had all been a couple of years ago, so he wanted to be certain he was totally on the ball when it came to trigger time.

Demeter City was a jumbled sprawl of crazy quilt architecture and alien design, a twisted willynilly parody of futuristic planning. Patchwork stuff, stupider than the cities of Earth, even that ever-teetering-upon-oblivion New York City. He didn't much care to be here, but the pay was good, and he was among the best at what he did. Anyway, it was good to move into new territory from time to time. It allowed the heat from the old hits to cool off for a while. And right now things were pretty damned hot for him on Earth, you bet.

Besides, there was a particular person he wanted to look up here on Demeter City. A blast from the past. Motivation above and beyond for this interstellar hop, no question.

He grinned around the cigarette.

He took the butt from his mouth, added one more puff of pollution, then buried the rest of the smoke in a tray. He folded the tray and placed it in the inside pocket of his black specialty jacket.

Thing was, these days—on Earth as well as here on the launching point into alien space—assassins tended to go for high-tech. That was okay, he supposed, but all those machines were complicated. Complicated things often didn't work the way they were supposed to.

In this profession, you couldn't really afford that margin of error.

Keep it simple.

That was his policy.

The more you kept hits simple and clean, the more likely you were to get away with them.

His nostrils twitched. There was a particularly acrid smell wafting around here, changing from the previous miasma. His trained eyes jerked about, taking in the panorama. Roof. Jutting bric-a-brac, chimneys, and tubings. No living creatures up here. Nothing to be concerned about. Some kind of new odor, jettisoned from a kitchen somewhere and brought here by a breeze. Still, you had to pay attention to every detail prefacing situations like these, and so the net of his senses was open wide to catch everything he could. For one little twitch of taste, smell, touch, sound, or sight could mean he had to abort and escape. This was why he had never been caught committing murder. He was more than a professional. He was an instinctive, natural, urban hunter, who brought to his trade every bit of grim talent a brilliant carnivore practices in the jungle.

He examined his sophisticated wrist chronometer.

Time.

The assassin lifted his weapon, flexed his arms,
and trained the scope sights down toward the
streets. Carefully, he tracked down a side alley,
finding the entrance he had walked past earlier,
calculating a good spot to shoot from, which
resulted in his perching on this ledge.

The key thing about assassinations wasn't
weapons. Weapons were easy. Skill was important,
no question. But the most vital element of the
whole bloody business was information. Facts,
schedules, times, and data. This was the material
that he demanded before he took on a job. This was
the material that he'd been given for this particular assignment, and he'd given it the hard study
and practice it deserved.

Zin Mooka was the mark's name. He was a
Tarn, some kind of CEO for a big company called
Oshgo Industries. Somehow Oshgo was connected
with crime figures, and somehow Zin Mooka had
run afoul of these dangerous men. It wasn't the
assassin's business to inquire into the actual
details, and he learned only the things about his
marks that it was necessary to learn for the purposes of the job. Otherwise, it was best to keep it
cut-and-dried. In. Kill. Out.

This CEO named Zin Mooka, the assassin
knew, had an appointment with a shady collabora-
tor at a place only a couple of miles away. For such
meetings, Zin Mooka would leave by the side

entrance and duck into a small, nondescript car which would drive him to his meeting. For perhaps three seconds, the mark would be well exposed to a bullet. Not much time, true—but time enough for a pro.

He did not have to wait long.

The door opened.

An associate stepped out, a Creon in a dark suit and tie. The Creon looked first right, then left, then stepped out and hailed something down the alley.

Within moments a groundcar rolled out.

The Creon opened the car door, then turned and gestured.

First out was a human, a man in another dark suit and tie. He got into the car.

Wait . . . thought the assassin. *Steady now . . .*

He concentrated. He placed his total being into the moment. Time seemed to slow. He and his weapon became one.

The Tarn walked out. Nor, fortunately, did he seem to be in a particular hurry. He walked out, stopped, looked around as though he was taking a big breath of outside. He was a short Tarn in a maroon jacket, with a ruffle at his throat. He looked well groomed and self-satisfied. In his hand he held a briefcase.

The shooter's finger stiffened on the trigger.

Then the unexpected happened.

Without warning, the Tarn businessman's eyes swung around and looked up. Straight up at the assassin. It was as though Zin Mooka were looking through the scope into the assassin's soul. His big Tarn eyes were wide with alarm and fear.

Less of a pro would have been so shocked he would have lost the moment. A split second after the mark looked up, he started leaping for cover.

The shooter tracked him, squeezing off two shots.

The first shot tore a divot out of the Tarn's chest.

Blood spattered back onto the sidewalk.

The second tore through the Tarn's third eye.

The mark went down.

The assassin went on automatic.

Quickly, he pushed himself back off the ledge, out of the line of sight. He packed up in practiced, quick moves, then headed out on his prearranged path down a staircase and into the depths of the building from whose roof he had committed his crime.

Thinking: *Damn.*

Later, with a little oxygen and rest in him, the assassin felt better.

He lay in the bed of his hotel room, his TV on, sound off.

He was sipping a drink, calming down, allowing himself a little time to blow out some of his mental agitation.

The Tarn must have somehow psyched his death. That was the problem with Tarns, yes, but the assassin had thought that at that distance it wouldn't be a difficulty. The psyching hadn't prevented him from pulling off the job, but that wasn't the issue. The assassin had been alarmed because the mark had looked up, seen some trace of him, received *some* kind of psychic impression. If he'd been able to transmit that information to a fellow Tarn, there might be a problem.

However, upon the reflection that time and a couple of bottles of chilled *darkan* brew brought, the assassin realized that there had been no time for that transmission. Dead Tarns aren't psychic, and he'd put the guy down quickly. Besides, there had been no other Tarns in the immediate vicinity.

The assassin brought the bottle to his lips, savoring the cold, yeasty refreshment his drink brought.

Clink. Whir.

Noises in his head. Disorientation. The room started to dissolve around him. He saw stars and planets. Alien landscapes of fire and ice. Majestic panoramas shunted within the space of a few moments and he lost track of his sense of self, his identity.

Damn! He hated it when this happened.

He gripped on to reality, forced himself back into proper ID mode. He replayed some of his memories like rosary beads.

The room shivered and settled back into place, and he realized he'd probably had too much to drink, so he pushed the *darkan* brew aside.

The phone rang.

Feeling human again, the assassin picked it up. "Yes?"

"Good effort," said a raspy voice.

"Thanks."

"We'd like you to consider another study."

"Study," of course, meaning "target."

"I'm always willing to continue my education. Who are we talking about here?"

"An individual in the Demeter City Police Department."

And then the voice told him who that was, and the details of the entire situation.

Officer Jane Castle
strode through the precinct corridor, steaming,
teeth clenched so hard that the sinews in her slender neck stood out like bands.

This whole thing *sucked*.

She'd been here *long* before Brogan and
Haldane. Now they were being inducted into some
kind of *Boys' Club*, for gosh sakes!

And Podly! For years she'd put up with that
man's abuse, hoping for just recognition. Now the
steak went to the guys and she got the scraps.

It was all too much, she thought as she stormed
down the corridor, nearly bumping into Orrin
(Creon: "Excuse me." Human: "Grunt.") and generally viewing the entire police parade in a haze of
red. She swept past klicks of files, swept past the
sausage and *yarn* potato smell of the commissary,

swept past the sound of flushing toilets of the LADIES', GENTLEMEN's, and OTHERS' rooms, the taste of sour grapes strong in her mouth.

Jane Castle had been tops, *number one, in her graduating class back in the Academia Polizia in New Europe.* Above the other women, above the other men. Her two years on the European Police were sterling examples of high brilliance performance. *That* was why she'd been tapped to be among the first to come to Demeter City to help with the policing there after the Big Contact from Galactic Central. She'd shone here as well, learning the strange ins and outs of a galactic city, learning different languages, learning to cope on her own—and then imparting to the Johnny-come-latelies like Brogan and Haldane her hard-won knowledge and experience. She long suspected there was something like this going on behind the scenes of Precinct 88, long thought that these alien people were keeping something from her. Try as she might, she never totally felt as at *home* as she wanted, as accepted.

Now the gold rings were being passed out to Brogan and Haldane. Not because they were the first or even the best of the Terran cops here, but because they happened to have arrows instead of pluses tacked onto their sexual symbols.

She'd heard the whole sad thing up there by Podly's office, just beyond their awareness, and the true scope and reality, the warp and woof, of the situation crashed down on her.

Sheeesh!

By the time Jane Castle reached Tech, a wild plan was beginning to come together in her mind.

Something had to be done. Within the Halls of Justice, Justice must finally be properly served!

Equality! No taxation without representation! *E pluribus unum* . . . et cetera, et cetera.

"Took!" cried Officer Jane Castle, spotting her friend at a station. "Took, I've got to talk to you immediately!"

Officer Took was a Tarn female police-person, and a good friend. For some reason, as soon as Jane had gotten to Demeter City—frightened but chipper and willing to take what was thrown at her—Took stepped in and placed her under her wing. Maybe it was her psychic mental abilities, but she'd known that it wasn't just knowledge that this new creature from a strange planet needed, but reassurance and understanding. However, as soon as Jane Castle started blooming, she became the dominant member of the friendship. It was always Jane who made the suggestions about what they would do, or where they would go, or what they would talk about. That was just Jane Castle's nature, and Tookie seemed to accept it as part and parcel of being her friend.

"Jane!" said Took as she looked up from the monitor where she was working. Her third eye— right above the limpid orbs of the other two, in the center of her smooth, elegant forehead—blinked with surprise. This lid wasn't open often—mostly it rose when Tarns used their telekinetic or other psychic powers. "What's going on?"

Jane plopped down in the chair beside her, frowning intently. "I'll tell you what's going on, Took. Injustice. Intolerance. Iniquity!"

"Of course, Jane. That's why we're here. To deal with all of that below on Demeter City." The aesthetically featured Tarn smiled patronizingly. One of Took's many good characteristics was her calm and her cool. Generally, Jane valued this. After all, Took was a good friend. Now, though, didn't seem to be an appropriate time for stoicism. Now was the time for barn-burning, rabble-rousing, and loosing the dogs of war.

Female dogs.

"No. It's going on *right here* in the precinct." Jane tapped the counter emphatically with her fingernails. "There's a conspiracy. A movement afoot to keep us women down. Underfoot. The moral equivalent of pregnant and in the galactic kitchen! It's time for liberation from the—"

"Are you talking about the GOKS?"

The name struck a chord in Jane.

"Yes. I believe that was the word that was being bandied about so brazenly!" she said.

"I shouldn't think it was so brazenly."

"Well, I suppose I did *overhear* it mentioned." Jane squinted at Tookie, confused. "You *know* about this arrogant exercise in outright chauvinism?"

"Yes. Certainly. The Gathering of Kindred Souls." Took smiled sweetly and complacently, folding her arms about her slim frame and tilting her head in a "So, what's the problem?" gesture.

"You're not *offended* by its very existence?"

"Why should I be?"

Jane Castle was taken aback. She huffed and reddened, her mind boggling at the concept of a modern woman, steeped and benighted in such cultural darkness.

"Because it's *wrong*, Took."

"Wrong?"

"Yes. Our rights are being trampled upon. Our sex is being slighted. It's . . . it's . . . I mean, Took. You work as hard as anyone here. But it would appear as though there's a secret society of back-slapping gladhanders who control the power here."

Took licked her lips thoughtfully. "My goodness, it's just a bunch of males who go to Dreek Island and give secret buttock bumps."

"Buttock bumps?"

"Oh, we're not supposed to know about those, we female cops. But we do."

"How long has this atrocity been tolerated?"

Took looked thoughtful, as though counting.

"Well, it was the Creons who started it, just like they started the police force. It's a part of Creon culture, and Tarns are pretty affable souls, so they just went along with it. So I guess it's always been around, Jane. I'm surprised you haven't noticed it before."

Jane Castle's nose and mouth twisted with disgust.

"Come to think of it, I *have* noticed discrimination from time to time. But I hardly felt comfortable pointing it out, being a representative of my planet and all. But now that Haldane and Brogan are jumping feet first into what amounts to a system that limits an important segment of the workforce, a group that holds *me* back from what *I* deserve—well, I have to do *something*."

Took pursed her lips thoughtfully. "For starters, perhaps you should have a seat and let me make you a cup of *sasha* tea. You know that always settles you down when you get a little bit excited. Like that time that Jack stole your underwear."

"The *pervert*," snapped Jane. "Took, maybe I just don't *want* to calm down."

"Well, please, Jane, I'm a bit mentally sensitive to the kind of psychic emanation you're giving off." Took rubbed a temple as though signaling a headache.

"Oh dear. I'm so sorry, Took." Jane Castle sighed. "I didn't mean to hurt you, Took."

"No harm done."

She sat in a chair. "Maybe I *should* have some of that tea."

She put her hands to her face to rub her eyes.

"I'll just be one second." Took stood and gracefully strode to the refreshment station in the corner. There she pressed some buttons on a converter. Jane Castle took a few more deep breaths and, by the time she was through, Took was holding a cup of aromatic liquid in front of her. Jane took it with thanks and sipped. Flowers and roots and stimulation. Alien mists and contemplative moods.

"See. It always works, doesn't it?" said Took

soothingly, as she sat back down, smoothing the crisp blue of her uniform.

"Well, my blood pressure may be down a bit, Took, but I quite assure you my dander is still up," said Castle. "I still must admit to being absolutely baffled by your calm acceptance of this GOKS business."

Took shrugged. "I have a busy life, a full life. I suppose I don't think too much about ancient customs. I guess I just always assume they're there for a reason."

"Oh, let me tell you—there's a reason for organizations like GOKS. Subjugation and abuse of women! On my planet only in the last century or so has feminine consciousness been raised enough to *try* and throw off that yoke. But it's a pernicious and insidious social phenomenon that must be fought at every turn, pulled out by its twisted, filthy roots!"

Took sat back, looking as though she'd taken a long ride off a short asteroid. "Goodness, Jane. I've never heard words like that. You truly are angry about this subject. Tea or no tea!"

"Took, I didn't get where I am today by making paper dolls." She smiled knowingly. "I used my scissors elsewhere!"

"Hmmm. Maybe I'd better get some tea for myself."

Jane leaned over, grabbed her knee. "That can wait. You have to tell me what you know about this GOKS thing."

Took shrugged. "What can I say. It's a place

where the boys go to let off some steam. Bond. Kill innocent creatures. Play *shrat*."

"*Shrat?*"

"I believe it's something like Earth golf."

"Country club. An *exclusive* country club. Well. This is insupportable, Took."

"I don't support it. You just sort of live with it. I will say, though, they go away crabby and they come back much happier. That makes things go a lot easier around here!"

"Hmm. Well, I can see I'm not going to get the goods on this evil organization by talking to you. Is there any other woman here who knows or cares more?"

"Not that I know of. I think we all agree, it's a good thing," said Took.

"How can you say a system that subjugates women is a good thing? Why, for instance, isn't there a *woman* captain here?"

"I suppose that no woman is crazy enough to want the job."

"Rationalization." Jane pondered. "It's clear that I'm not going to be able to collect the facts from you or from the other women . . ." She chuckled humorlessly. "And certainly not from the men here."

"No. It's secret."

"Yes, and *well* it should be. But it's a relic of the past that should not be allowed to continue into a politically correct future galaxy."

"Politically correct?"

"Definitions later, Took. No, I can see this is going to have to be a case of investigative journalism. I'm going to blow the cover off of this egregious practice.

They may ship me back to Earth, but I don't care. I have to make the galaxy an equal place for females . . ."

"But Jane—"

"Shush, Took. I'm thinking." She put a finger into the air. "There's only one way. Took, do you know where this Dreek Island is?"

"Uhm . . . no. Someplace in an ocean somewhere, I suppose."

Jane got up, paced.

As it happened, the precinct robot, a roundish rolling thing resembling nothing so much as a high-tech trash can wearing its lid a little high, chose that moment to enter.

"Slomo!"

The head canted.

"Officer Castle. What can I do for you?"

"Slomo. I have access to your data banks, true?"

Colored lights blinked for just a second. "That's very true. You are an officer here, and you have access to all pertinent knowledge I can plug into."

Jane pointed the neighboring interface module. "Get thee hence and plug!"

Obediently, Slomo the robot approached the conduit. An extensor extruded and fitted neatly into a square hole. Something clicked and Slomo's lights blinked sequentially in the opposite direction.

Jane was about to ask about GOKS and Dreek Island, but suddenly realized that all this was classified in a way that Slomo could have no access to: hidden in the little pea brains of men.

However, there *was* another way.

"Slomo, a criminal has escaped to a place called Dreek Island. Do you have access to information on this place?"

"Dreek Island. Processing." A wink, a blink. "Ah yes, a tropical island in the Miltaz Sea."

"I need a printout. All information. Longitude, latitude. Transportation access. Flora, fauna. Golf courses."

"Golf courses, Officer Castle?"

"Never mind on that one, Slomo. Just give me a printout."

"No problem, sweetheart."

"Oh no. Not you too, Slomo. Must all males be sexist pigs?"

Slomo beeped and whistled, a sure sign of robotic vexation. "I was not aware I had any sex, Officer Castle."

"You're a male by default, Slomo. Doubtless you were programmed by males, true?"

"I believe so."

"Your voice is male."

"Ah. Yes, that is true. However, I have no other sexual characteristics."

"Hmm. True. And as for the rest—well, nobody's perfect. Well then. Slomo, I hereby dub you an honorary female. I'd knight you with my nightstick if I had one. You get the idea, though."

"I'm very honored," piped the robot.

"Good. Now. That printout if you please."

With a flurry of clicker clacking, the robot commenced his printout while Jane looked on with approval.

"Pardon me, Jane," said Took. "I generally respect others' privacy, but my psychic faculties cannot help but detect a tremor in my Big Trouble Detector. You wouldn't—"

"—be planning something, Took? As a matter of fact, I am. And you, fellow female, must help me."

Took looked troubled. "Me? Why me. I'm hardly one to rock the boat, Jane."

"Then your consciousness must be raised, Tookie. You must see the light."

"Just what are these plans?"

"It's quite simple, Tookie. You see, if I merely start whining about inequality on the police force, I'll be labeled by the news media and Inner Affairs and the courts as just another troublesome female— *and* I'll probably be shipped back to Earth." She took a firm stand and lifted a finger indignantly into the air. "However, if I accumulate hard irrefutable evidence of these dire circumstances and conspiracies—namely through photographs, recordings, and corroborative eyewitnesses—then I can expose these practices and perhaps even eradicate them . . . and maintain my hard-won position here."

"You won't be very popular."

"Unpopularity I can stand it . . . It's happened to me before." She gave a pixieish smile. "It never lasts for long. Anyway, there's always the possibility of merely *threatening* to expose this little Boys' Club . . . That may be just enough leverage to crack it, make it coed, so to speak."

"I don't know, Jane. I don't know if I want anything to *do* with the GOKS."

"Of course you do! Power! They're the ones who hold the power here. That's what we need more of, you and I and other valuable females who work for this honorable establishment. We deserve respect and equality."

"Your printout, Officer Castle."

"Thank you, Slo—Hmm . . . Perhaps with your new sex change we should call you Slo*ma*."

"That would be acceptable."

"Excellent." Jane retrieved the printout. Included was a map. She examined this cursorily. "This looks reachable in a hopper."

"I believe it is, Officer Castle," said the robot.

Jane spun around to face Took. "Tookie. You've got lots of leave and sick days accumulated, right?"

"I hardly ever use them . . . I *like* to work."

"Well, consider this work, then."

"When would this be, Jane?" asked Took uneasily.

"Next week, just about the time Haldane and Brogan take their little Boys' Club jaunt—We'll take a little trip ourselves to this Dreek Island." Her eyes fairly glowed with dignity and valiant purpose. "And we'll find out exactly what's going on!"

Took blanched.

Jane Castle, Woman of the Year.

No, strike that. Jane Castle, Woman of the Century. Perhaps there were would be *books* written about her, for future women to model themselves on . . . Susan B. Anthony . . . Germaine Greer . . . Drew Barrymore . . . Jane Castle!

She sat at her desk the printout of the Dreek Island details stretched out before her.

A headline spun in her head: CASTLE NAMED CHIEF OF INTERGALACTIC POLICE. Another: CASTLE RECEIVES YET MORE HIGH HONORS. And yet another: BRILLIANT POLICEWOMAN RECEIVES YET MORE HONORS.

Jane smiled to herself.

A woman, after all, had to have *goals*.

Her MultiCom rang, snapping her out of her exalted reverie.

"Castle," she said.

"Jane?" A man's voice. Familiar. "How are you?" Friendly.

"It's Ted Bickford. I'm back on Demeter City and I'd *love* to see you."

Jane Castle's heart beat harder.

CHAPTER

Brogan had seen worse.

Some blood and brains on the sidewalk and walls, the dead guy wrapped up, the chalk outline vivid against the grey of concrete. Could have been a splash of real life from the Big Bad Apple. Except it was thousands of light-years north of the East River.

The MultiCom-unit Captain Podly carried bawled for attention.

"Right here," said Podly, glowering at the assassination scene with infinite distaste.

"Found the site, sir. About where you figured."

Brogan looked up toward the building and the site they'd triangulated, Haldane following his gaze.

"Whew. Pure skilled professionalism," said his partner, pushing his hat back and scratching his dark locks with resignation.

"M.O. doesn't seem consistent with normal Demeter City procedure on these sorts of things," said Brogan, eyes scouring the scene, trying to catch some missing piece of the puzzle that had been overlooked.

"And get this, sir," continued the remote MultiCom voice. "The analyzer shows trace Earth gunpowder residue."

"Hmm. Earth rifle. Difficult to master, but effective," said Podly. "Ejected shells?"

"No sir. Very clean," barked the Multicom.

"I want you to go over that roof with a fine-tooth *glintz* comb," said Podly. "And then do it again. I want to catch this bastard before he pulls this kind of stunt again."

Haldane gave a significant look at Brogan, who nodded.

Looked like someone had brought in an Earth assassin for this one. If that was the case, the hit would be clean, the killer would lie low again, and then, weeks from now, he'd quietly take a ship to New Hawaii to get a tan before returning to the Green Hills of Home. What *they* were going to have to do was to check incoming humans for the last month or so and then match them up with their latest Known Criminals file from Terra CompCentral. It would take a little time, but it was the only way they'd have any hope of catching a hoodlum of this caliber, so to speak.

Haldane stepped over beside his partner and whispered *sotto voce*. "I wonder if he's more upset about the killing—or the crimp the investigation might put on his holiday."

"I heard that," said Podly quietly. He stepped over to the duo. "Get this straight. I'm a dedicated policeman. This case is going to be solved and the perp *will* be brought to justice."

Haldane stiffened, blanching. "Yes sir."

"But there's no way *scum* like this is going to ruin our special time together. So we'll just work as hard as possible with the time we have available. It's not like we'll be incommunicado. We can always come back if necessary."

Podly patted them both on the back, then returned to talk to the forensic scientist.

Haldane waited until he was sure the captain was out of earshot before he spoke again.

"See what I mean?"

Brogan scratched behind his ear. "Not like Podly. He snaps onto a case like this, he hangs on like a Doberman pinscher."

"Did you have any doubt since he let us in on the GOKS that he's obsessed on the subject?"

Brogan watched as his colleagues made speedy work of the crime scene. Passersby lingering by the crime scene tape were ushered along their way. Media were expelled with promises of a press conference soon, full disclosure of facts, and all the official pictures they cared to print. Hokum, of course. A proper investigation could not be conducted by revealing *all* facts to the press, especially the sensational tabloids that proliferated on Demeter City. However, you had to throw them *some* kind of bone, and the Demeter cops had long since learned how to keep things under wraps as much as possible.

"I wouldn't say obsessed," said Brogan. "As much as enthusiastic." He bent down and examined a speck of what could be bone matter in the corner between the sidewalk and building. "You know, Podly's been working damned hard for a long, long time. I daresay he deserves a break once in a while, right?" He smiled grimly. "Come to think of it, maybe *we* do too." He took a handkerchief out and rubbed the sweat off his brow. It was a hot day, and the streets were cooking beneath the haze that cloaked the mammoth city. "I love my wife and kids, you know that, Jack. But I've been thinking—a few days away, sporting on a pleasant island somewhere—how bad can that be?"

"Great, if it was with some willowy blonde and an expense account," said Haldane. "We're going to be cooped up with a bunch of Creons and Tarns. *Male* Creons and Tarns. God knows what's going to happen." He sighed. "I'm relegating it to duty time, Patrick. Vacation time I'm going to spend *off* planet—I promise you that."

"Just trying to be positive, Jack. Give it a chance. Sounds like you're pretty stressed-out, and this could be the opportunity to let some of that tension go."

"Stressed-out. You bet. But like I said, if there were some attractive human females on this Dreek Island place, I'd feel a lot better about the whole thing."

Brogan felt a little peeved. "So you're not into the whole idea of male bonding—participating in a breakthrough in alien–human relationships."

"When you put it that way, I guess I am, Patrick. But we were talking about personal feelings. I'm just saying it doesn't sound like much of a vacation to me."

Brogan thought about that for a moment. "Sometimes a change can be as good as a rest, Haldane."

Jack grinned. "Hey. You just made that up right now, huh? You're pretty good, partner."

"Actually I have a team of writers working night and day to impress you, Jack." He folded his arms over his chest, surveyed the scene once more. "So. Earth assassin, imported by who?"

"Somebody with money."

"Obviously. Serious money. We're also going to have to ask a few questions of the departed's company. Get a little background on his dealings."

"Good luck to us on that," said Haldane, resignation in his voice. "These alien corporations are pretty convoluted."

"Yeah. I know," said Brogan absently. On a hunch he stepped around the side of a building and looked around. Up and down the street, the gutter . . ."

"I'll start Jane on the process."

A few feet from the corner, below the lip of a curb, in the drainage slough, something shone.

Brogan bent over, picked it up.

It looked like some kind of asymmetrical gem. White and blue, with a cat's-eye twist in the center. Like a geometrically warped child's marble but smaller.

"Jack. Take a look at this?" said Brogan, standing up and offering his partner a look.

"Hmm. Looks odd and alien. Imagine finding something odd and alien on a planet zillions of light-years from Earth."

"You think it's got something to do with this death?"

"I don't see how. It's not a bullet. Trajectory's wrong for it to have spilled out of the dead guy's pocket. I think you've just found something that someone else lost."

"Hmmm. Kinda pretty, kinda weird. Got a strange vibration to it. Feel."

"Oh no, I've had my fill of Tarn psychic power stuff for a while."

"Guess I'd better take it back, just in case." He took out a plastic bag, inserted the skewed gem, stuck it in his pocket, and continued his scouring of the territory.

You never knew where you were going to find the clue that would crack a case.

CHAPTER

Jane Castle was
stunned.

If anything, the man looked more handsome
than ever.

That twinkle in those big blue eyes, that gor-
geous curly blond hair, immaculately shaped
around his perfect features. That cute nose . . .

She drank in the look of him even as she sat
down at the table, her defenses already crum-
bling.

"Hello, Ted," she said, softly, working hard not
to betray the way just seeing him, just being in his
vicinity, upped her heart rate.

"Hi, Jane. I'm glad you could see me so soon."
He smiled, revealing impeccably white teeth. Turned
a hand, palm up, presenting the seat opposite
him.

They were dining in the Chez Meteor, a fancy French—Demeter City place that attempted to combine European cooking with local ingredients for the upwardly mobile human population of this galactic crossroads and the curious alien rich.

He had taken her there once before, when she'd been homesick for Earth. It had been the best date of her life.

She sat down, feeling disappointed. He hadn't gotten up to kiss her or anything familiar. True, that would not have been at all appropriate, given the present circumstances of their relationship— or, rather *non*-relationship. However, it would have been nice to be able to turn a proffered kiss down . . .

And even nicer, she realized now with her physical reaction to him, to accept it.

"It's been too long, Jane," he said, pouring her some champagne from a bucket by the side of the table.

"Two years without any communication, yes," she said. "I would have written or sub-spaced or *something,* Ted, if I had an address. You *did* promise me an address."

He held up his hands with despair. "When does a freelancer like me ever have an address?" He smiled glumly, looking totally miserable at having given her any pain whatsoever. Jane had had every intention of telling the guy off even before *hors d'oeuvres,* but how could she when her heart was melting at the sight of him, and all the memories of their good times together were popping up in her mind?

"Oh, surely you have *some* base of operations," she said, managing to inject a bit of her trademark tartness into her words and proud of herself for hurdling all the treacle in her heart.

"Strikes me that an engineering consultant could engineer himself a simple post office box."

"Jane! Not only have I been traveling all over Earth—I've been hopping about *planets*. My kind of engineering is very much in demand these days and—" He sighed. "God, you look beautiful tonight." He reached across the table and took her hand in his strong, big hands. "You're right, I've been awful. A thoughtless bastard. I don't know how I could have neglected writing you—or something. I guess"—he sighed, looking down at the beautifully set table, at his full glass of champagne, bubbles winking at the top—"I guess maybe I was trying to suppress my feelings. Trying to make light of them. That's the way I operate sometimes, I suppose." He shook his head mournfully. "I don't think I'm going to be able to eat tonight unless I think there is a slim chance of your forgiving me."

She raised an eyebrow, sipped her champagne, seeming to give the whole issue some serious thought. In actuality, she'd forgiven him the moment he called, but she couldn't let him know that. She'd let him wriggle a bit.

"I'll give you just enough forgiveness," she said

dryly, "to allow you to peck forlornly at some cheese."

He laughed. "Ah, Jane. You're *such* a big sweetheart. I knew you'd forgive me. When I came to Demeter City I just had to see you, and it was hard to know that I was going to have to suffer your anger . . . But it's worth it." He picked up his glass and clinked it against hers. "Here's to open hearts."

"Here's to open-heart surgery if you *dare* not to write again," she said.

He laughed. "Now then, here's your menu. Shall we order?"

She quaffed her glass of bubbly first and had another before she could even think of picking out what she wanted. She was relieved that this was going so well, but she was still a little heartsick, remembering the state Ted Bickford had left her in, and the lonely wait for some communication from him.

She'd met him at an Earthers' club here on Demeter City. Ted was a special project engineer who'd been shipped in to try to straighten out some of the messes here on Demeter City, and to consult in some of the expansions that were being planned. She'd been here awhile and was having a slightly hard time of it.

Jane Castle had been the belle of the European ball back in Europe. She'd had plenty of boyfriends, plenty of dates. There had been only one fellow she'd been serious about, but that was back in the Police Academy, and the competition had been just too much for the relationship. This was why she now had such a hard time even considering getting emotionally involved with another police officer. (Of course, she wouldn't get involved with that arrogant puppy Jack Haldane if he were the last human male in the Universe, cop badge or no cop badge.) She'd known there would be few human males to choose from for company, out here on Demeter City. It didn't seem to matter at the time. The opportunity was too vast, and her ambition was overwhelming. However, as the months wore on, her excitement with her job did not abate—but her sense of emotional invulnerability did.

It was long past this point when she'd met Ted.

It had been a whirlwind romance. He'd been on Demeter City for only a month, and had been very honest about where the limitations had to be placed on the circumstances of their involvement.

Yes, yes, of course: she'd understood, totally. With her mind, that was. A girl needs a romantic fling from time to time, that mind told her. Romantic trysts by Oshnar Falls on the southern peninsula. Picnics and poetry in the Azure Fields.

A beautiful room in the Space Suites, with a floor full of stars. Champagne in a hot tub.

Unfortunately, her heart had jumped in far deeper than her mind. So, when that mind casually said *au revoir* to this handsome, hunky paramour, chalking up a good time and a conquest most glorious, she thought she could deal with it. Her heart, however, ached for months afterward. And when no billet-doux showed, that heart sank lower and lower.

She'd survived, of course, and actually was grateful for the boot camp training in lost love. It hardened her just enough to be more cynical, she reasoned.

Now, though, that she was sitting with him, the smell of cologne and maleness tickling her nose and sensuality, she felt her heart slowly rising up from the grave, light streaming forth, the heavens ringing majestically. She was feeling again, in a way she hadn't for a while.

She didn't know if this was good or bad. All she knew was that, goddammit, she was very happy to see Ted Bickford, communications or no.

They ordered salads and a good wine, and then a simple bouillabaisse of local seafood. At Chez Meteor it was best to keep it simple.

When they'd given their menus to the *garçon*, Ted grabbed up her hand again.

"God, it's good to see you again."

"Please. *Goddess*."

He laughed. He was dressed simply in a dark jacket and a faux-tie shirt, but his well-proportioned body with large shoulders and narrow waist gave it all the class of a tuxedo. Being in close proximity to him unlocked all kinds of memories and opened up something inside Jane Castle that she realized was a spark of hope. She kept it all under rigid control, however.

"How *are* you doing in your police duties? You know, I've always admired your strength and abilities in that really difficult area."

She smiled sardonically. "Well, Demeter City's *always* a problem to deal with."

"A regular hotbed of crime, eh?"

"Things haven't changed since you were here last, that's for sure."

"Ah yes. Murder, chicanery, larceny, bootlegging, racketeering, mugging, robbery, illegal drugs, vice . . . The whole laundry list of Earth crimes . . . And some new ones, as I recall."

"We cope."

"I'm just so impressed that you've been able to keep on here, despite it all."

"It's my duty. I take duty very seriously, that and commitment."

"I know, Jane. And that's one of your many, many precious qualities." He scratched his nose thoughtfully. "I'm a little confused, though. With your ambition and abilities so obvious, I would have thought I'd be having dinner with at least a corporal by now!"

Her eyes flared. "Yes! You'd think so, wouldn't you!"

"Wow. Nice to see that anger directed at something other than my lack of communication abilities. What the hell's been going on?"

She took another drink of champagne, and he happily refilled her glass. "I'll tell you what's been going on! Inequality! This planet is badly in need of affirmative action!"

"No!"

"It's true. I've said nothing about my lack of promotion. I realize that it's been busy here, and I'm a

newcomer to this police force, relatively speaking."
She put bite and pith into her words, relishing the
opportunity to unleash anger in a way that
wouldn't be threatening to him. "But today has
been the absolute last straw."

"What happened?"

Bread and pâté arrived and they took a moment
to assemble their food and take a few bites. Then
she told him the whole sad story.

"No! Sounds like something out of nineteenth
century Earth. It's barbaric!"

"You bet it is. And I'm going to change
things. I don't care what happens . . . If they
send me back to Earth . . . Well, that's just the
way it goes. I simply can't abide this kind of
inequality."

"Good for you!"

She had expected him to act like every other
man: namely, defensively. Even liberal-minded
men, in her experience, had a male-centric core.
Ted was a no-nonsense, let's-get-business-done-
and-enjoy-the-good-things-of-life kind of guy,
though. Come to think of it, although he was in
most respects an athletic man's-man kind of
guy—interested in sports, gambling, and fast
cars—she really had never heard him be anything
but respectful toward females and their quest for
equality and respect. Come to think of it, this was
one of the reasons she'd been attracted to him.
(Psychologically, anyway—the other reasons
she'd been drawn to Ted had nothing to do with
his politics.)

"You agree with me?"

"Absolutely." He put his hand on hers reassuringly. "When you put your life on the line all the time as you do, Jane, you deserve the same treatment and opportunities *anyone* gets in that precinct station."

"Yes. That's what I honestly believe too," said Jane, very grateful for the support from this unexpected source. "Thank you so much for saying that, Ted."

"It's what I sincerely believe. And you're right. I know men. I'm one. When you get us together in a group, we're absolutely insufferable."

"I'll say."

"That's one of the reasons I'm a loner, Jane. I'm really often ashamed of the antics of my sex." He looked thoughtful as he leaned his head into his hands for a moment. "Look. I owe you. I've got a few days off next week. I honestly was hoping to spend some of that time seeing you anyway—presumptuous, I know—but there you are. With my military experience, I would think I'd be pretty good on this kind of undercover operation you have planned. I agree—accumulating this kind of evidence is vital in presenting your case." He paused for effect, turning his sincere baby blues on her. "I'd like to volunteer to go on this trip with you. I'm sure I could help. I mean, I'm sure you're fully capable of doing it yourself, but you never know how a handy guy like me might be put to good use!"

She stared at him, surprised and delighted.

Ted was right. He *would* be a lot of help. What luck!

"I accept!" she said. "And maybe if you do a good job, I'll finish forgiving you for a certain lack of correspondence."

"That's rather what I had hoped," Ted Bickford said sheepishly.

"Hot dogs and hamburgers are up!" called Patrick Brogan, pushing the tilting chef's hat out of his eyes and fanning away the barbecue smoke from his face. Coughing. "Altorian chicken's taking a little longer than expected, I'm afraid."

The kids didn't seem to mind. "Hot dog for me, Dad," said fifteen-year-old Matt, hurrying up to his father and offering one paper plate topped with one bare hot dog bun.

Hurrying up beside him was twelve-year-old Liz with a similar plate, only this one bore a round bun. "Hamburger for me, Dad." She'd already placed a slice of onion, a piece of lettuce, and equal squirts of mustard and ketchup.

"Hey, Liz—hope you brought some Breath Killer along. That onion slice's pretty huge!" said Matt.

"Nope. And I'm going to breathe right in your face afterward!" said Liz.

Alas, daughter Liz had not exactly reached her ladylike phase yet. Of course, when she did she'd start dating, and Brogan wasn't sure he'd ever be prepared for that.

"Kids. Can you save your hostilities for the work week?" asked Sally Brogan, calling from the picnic table. "This is supposed to be a fun family outing."

By a great deal of finagling, and no small amount of providential luck, they'd managed to combine Brogan's day off from the force, Sally's day off from her job, and Liz and Matt's time off from school, and thus have some time to themselves. They chose to go out for a family picnic in People's Park, a tamed area of wilderness many miles from the choke and bustle of Demeter City. One area had just been planted with Earth-type trees, hurried up in growth by a special horticultural process, in honor of the humans who had moved to Altor. Picnic tables and barbecues had been built, and they'd had to reserve it weeks in advance. Brogan thought it was a good idea occasionally to remind his children of their cultural heritage.

Brogan proudly doled out his carefully prepared treats.

"Yuk. Looks kinda *burned,* Dad," said Liz.

"It's *barbecued,* dear, not burned," said Brogan.

"I hate to agree with her," said Matt, examining his own chunk of meat suspiciously. "But it *is* sort of black, Dad."

"Old American tradition. Trust me, they'll be

delicious," said Brogan, trying hard not to betray a slight feeling of annoyance. Cripes, when *he* was a kid, he took what his old man portioned out and was happy for it. Kids these days! Worse, intergalactic kids! Well, he'd done his best to make sure they remembered where they came from.

Sally had the table all decked out properly, from red-checked plastic cover and paper plates to Tupperware full of potato salad, macaroni salad, and salad salad, as well as coolers of cold drink.

All they lacked were ants.

Patrick Brogan was not particularly eager to get the Altorian equivalent. Probably about ten feet high, with scythelike pincers, that ate humans for lunch, if he knew the local fauna. No, he wasn't particularly eager to go hunting things on Dreek Island . . . Chances were the tables could too easily be turned. Which reminded him, he had to talk to Sally about what was happening this week: namely, that he wouldn't be home for four straight nights.

He waited until they were settled down and had eaten most of their lunch. "Not bad, Dad," said Liz. "But isn't carbonized food a cause of cancer?"

"Life's the major cause of cancer, dear," said Brogan. "Now enjoy."

"Patrick," said Sally. "Is that wise?"

"Is what wise?"

"Criticizing Liz for being health conscious."

"After years of eating junk, Liz chooses the family barbecue to worry about?" said Brogan.

"Boy, you should see what she keeps in her

locker at school! They call her the Candy Kid," said Matt.

Liz put her nose in the air. "I'll have you all know that I've turned over a new leaf. I've ditched the candy. Vitamins and nutrition are my new enthusiasms." She sniffed her cup of drink. "Mother, is this fresh-squeezed fruit juice?"

"I'm sorry, darling. It's Kook-Aid. Your favorite."

"My *former* favorite."

Her mother frowned. "Drink it, dear. We'll talk about this new nutrition kick tomorrow."

Brogan smiled around his juicy hamburger and winked at his son. Matt winked back, giggling to himself.

Ah, yes, the glories of a family gathering!

He'd played catch with his kids. Liz was just as good as Matt. He just wished they had girls' Little League here. She'd tear it all up. Maybe she'd get a sports scholarship back on Earth and save the old man some serious money.

They were good kids, he guessed. Matt was gangly and towheaded. Liz was a brunette and just showing the signs of pubescence (and fortunately had long since learned the Facts of Life from her voracious reading). He loved them, no question, but they were definitely precocious and intelligent and from time to time a bit smart-alecky. When he'd complain about it to Sally, she just pointed out that, from what she'd heard from his family, this was exactly the way he'd been when *he* was a teenager. Alas, all too true. Still, life with these kids could be easier.

After eating, they'd maybe play a game of cards and then take a walk and throw some Frisbee or lie down on a blanket and watch the sunset. Something bonding, something together. Something breathing in some fresh air as a family instead of bundled inside that Space Suburb. He certainly didn't want Liz and Matt to grow up agoraphobic.

The food was delicious and he had a warm, full feeling as he finished the piece of Altorian cherry pie that Sally had baked herself.

Well, best to get on with it.

He took a swallow of Kook-Aid (grape/apple/*gara* bulbs—tart and tangy) and then made his little announcement.

"Looks as though I'll be away most of the week on business, Sally."

"Oh." She looked up from her unfinished pie, with a surprised and "Now-you-tell-me?" kind of expression. "You're going to another planet?"

"Hey, cool. Which one, Dad?" asked Matt.

"As a matter of fact, no," said Brogan matter-of-factly. "Podly just sprang this on me, I'm afraid. It's a training thing. Out on an island somewhere."

"And you can't go during the day and come back home to bed at night?" said Sally.

"I'm afraid not. It's a twenty-four-hour-a-day indoctrination sort of thing. Podly figures it's time for Jack and me to go through it."

"Awesome, Dad. Are you going to wear camouflage and muck around in the mud and stuff?" asked Matt. "Can I come?"

"Yuck. Gross!" said Liz.

"I honestly don't know," said Brogan, looking chagrined at the very thought. "I'll let you know when I get back."

"Podly, huh?" said Sally, with a certain look she got sometimes.

Sally was a pretty, curly-haired blonde, with a pleasing slight roundness to her features and form that Brogan found eminently huggable. Generally she was sweet sunshine and soft smiles—but, from time to time, she got cynical, and when she did she was usually right. At those times she got this kind of look on her face—as if she'd just gotten a whiff of something rotten on Demeter City.

"I don't suppose that this could have anything to do with *golf* could it?" she said.

"Oh, Mom," said Liz. "Creons and Tarns don't play golf. I don't know of any alien beings here that play."

"Yeah, they've got sims for humans, and they're talking about putting some greens down here in this park," said Matt. "But Liz is right."

Sally arched an eyebrow. "That's not quite what I meant."

"What are you talking about, Mom?"

"Yeah? Is this some kind of code or something?"

"Your father used to play golf back on Earth, right, dear? Only that was a euphemism."

"I know what euphemisms are!" said Liz, eyes wide and eager. "They're *naughty*."

"Well, I don't think what we've got here is naughty," said Sally, laughing a bit. "Bless him, your dad's too much of a straight arrow for 'naughty.'"

"Oh, thanks, Sally. My kids won't look up to me now," lamented Brogan, poignantly.

"No, what I think we've got here is a little rite of passage for Jack and Patrick. It's my guess that it's just like back on Earth. We're seeing the Police Men's Club rear its warty face, hmmm?"

That was one big problem with Sally. What she couldn't ferret out with her considerable intelligence, she nailed with her amazing intuition. He hardly ever bothered to hide things from her—it was simply no use. So now it was quite a relief to be able to come clean.

"I guess I wanted to talk to you about that, yes."

"Glacial! A men's club?" said Matt. "You mean, like no smart-ass little sisters to plague you?"

Liz stuck her tongue out defiantly.

"Or wives or girlfriends or fellow female officers," said Sally.

"Dad has a girlfriend?" said Liz.

"Only you, pumpkin." He turned to his wife. "I'm afraid that's the scoop. I'm not particularly keen on going, but Podly is absolutely insistent. The nice thing, I guess, is that it *is* an honor, and it *is* a breakthrough in human–alien relations."

"Sounds like a triumph in male chauvinism to me!" said Liz.

Brogan held up his hands. "What am I supposed to do?"

"You can always stand up for what you think is right," said his wife in a soft voice. "You could gently explain to Podly that where you come from, females are honored as equals and that you think that this Space Precinct should think about becoming more progressive." She sighed. "Of course, then you'll probably be 86'd and put on latrine duty."

"Wow. Dad on latrine duty. What a concept," said Matt, shaking his head with wonder.

"Hey, Dad . . ." said Liz. "While you're in a cleaning mode, could you do my room? Mom's on my butt a lot about it."

"Children," said Sally, an edge in her voice. "We're having a serious and emotional political discussion here."

Uh-oh, thought Matt. *Are we taking a trip to PC City here?* It wasn't exactly his favorite place. He couldn't argue with the logic and values of political correctness, but it sure made him feel uncomfortable.

Matt and Liz did not feel even vaguely contrite. However, they did shut their mouths.

"Look, I'm even less comfortable about this than I was about the stuff I did with the guys back in New York," said Brogan defensively. "But what am I supposed to do? Podly just kind of bulldozed me into it. It's very seldom I see him smiling—and he just beamed all over the place at the thought. I mean, this hasn't been easy duty, working our way into the ranks of a police force on a different planet. Only thing we figure we can do is to go along for the ride and just see what happens."

He braced himself for the onslaught.

"I think that's just what you should do, dear," said his wife.

"Huh?" Brogan looked up, surprised. Macaroni salad plopped from his plastic fork onto the plate.

"Look, I'm not saying I approve. But you are in a difficult position, and you have a wonderful opportunity to get closer to Podly and the other Creons and Tarns. Male bonding and all that."

"Oooh. Sounds absolutely icky," said Liz, who shut up as soon as admonishing eyes turned her way.

"Now mind you, I can't promise to hold my tongue when we finally get Podly to come over for dinner one night. I think everyone has a right to speak their minds," said Sally. "But as for a men's club . . . Well, here's an opportunity to venture into alien territory . . . I say, grab it." She smiled. "Just don't have *too* good a time with all these fun-loving Tarn and Creon males. Don't forget to come back."

"Yeah, and bring some souvenirs, Dad," said Matt. "A shrunken head or two."

Brogan smiled, relaxing. Not exactly a blessing, but sweet understanding. At least if he botched this whole thing, he knew he had a good home to come back to.

CHAPTER

Mom and Dad were packing up the hopper. Matt was off tormenting a nest of bugs somewhere in the new oak forest. Liz was on her back, on a swath of grass where the family had just played Frisbee, looking at the clouds, daydream-dancing with them.

It was tough being a preteenager on an alien planet. Liz could bury herself in books and computer games with the best of them, but still, once in a while, life got her down. Lately, for instance . . .

Lately, she had a crush.

His name was Brian. Brian Minton, son of a computer whiz executive. He had long curly black eyelashes, deep brown eyes, and just the cutest dimples. He also, natch, didn't know that Liz existed. Well, that was the way he acted, anyway.

Why, oh why, did she have to live in the middle of the stupidest teenage cliché in the *Universe?*

It was so unfair. She knew all the sociological, anthropological, and biological ins and outs, but they didn't answer a major riddle.

Namely, how come when females started realizing that boys were cute because the girls' hormones had started maturing them, and their brains started humming and buzzing with life and feminine vitality, males were still picking their noses and fighting in the sandlot.

Figuratively speaking, of course. Brian was about her age, and he wasn't stupid or anything. He just wasn't looking at life the same way she was. So what was she supposed to do. Sneak up behind him and give him testosterone injections. Eeukk, anyway. Probably just make him grow hair all over his cute little body. The notion was too horrific to entertain seriously. So here was Liz Brogan, doing the two-step with some alien cumulus. Brainy Brogan, the ultimate tomboy herself, having pleasant airy-fairy thoughts about kissing a boy.

"Liz!" called her mother. "We're about ready to go."

"Okay, okay." She rolled over, thoughtfully examining another, smaller, friendlier-looking cloud. She felt something hard under her. Annoyed she moved and looked down at it.

It looked like some sort of rock. Pretty, too. No, not a rock. Some kind of pretty rock-jewel. You never knew what you were going to find on an alien planet. All kinds of different geology. She picked it up. The thing had an odd feel to it. She wondered what it was. She thought vaguely about showing it to Dad or Mom (certainly not to Matt! he'd steal it or drop it or something dumb).

She stuck the rock-jewel into her pocket.

Then Brian Minton swam back into her thoughts.

"Liz," he said. "Would you go steady with me and kiss me blind every night."

"You bet, Brian!" she answered.

"Hey! Slowpoke! Let's roll. Don't forget, you've got some serious TV watching slated for tonight," boomed her dad.

"Oh. Right!"

Liz Brogan got up and skipped back to her departing family, forgetting all about the odd thing she'd put into her pocket and totally ignoring a small, empty plastic bag whipping away in the breeze. Her imaginary lips still fastened onto Brian Minton's adorable face.

CHAPTER

"There it is," said Captain Podly, pointing down through the cruiser window proudly. "Dreek Island!"

Jack Haldane craned his neck over the Tarn pilot's shoulder to look down as the vehicle lowered over the vast bowl of aquamarine that was the ocean. The watery surface, flecked with only slight bits of wave foam on this sunny day, gave way on the horizon to a large clot of land rearing up as though in defiance of the sea. Rough rocky coast. Lots of jungle green. And off to the far side, a rise of craggy mountains.

"Looks more like Skull Island to me," said Haldane.

"What's that?" said Podly.

"Oh, a silly reference to an old Earth movie," said Brogan. "Pay him no mind, sir. We're really and truly happy to see it and excited about the whole prospect."

Still and all, thought Haldane, *if I see a huge ape named Kong knocking down trees, I'm going to want to catch the next hopper out of here.*

Haldane wasn't totally at ease with this scenario. It felt—skewed. Now, if this was a getaway retreat with a bunch of other normal *human* guys, that would be a different story. If this were Earth, you could be sure that there'd be another island close by that had only human gals. In that kind of situation, Haldane could not only enjoy the company of other normal joes like himself—but organize a panty raid!

No, he thought as he stared apprehensively at the growing misty and mysterious island. An island full of male Creons and Tarns, and God alone knew what else, just didn't have the same impact on his sense of place in the Universe. Hazing was one thing. Haldane had endured his at his college fraternity with equanimity. At least there, he knew that he had rewards waiting at the other end—plenty of parties, and a feeling of belonging. To say nothing of sorority browsing. Maybe that was the problem. The idea of alien hazing was unpleasant enough. The notion of an eventual sorority hop just did not appeal.

He'd mentioned this in passing to Brogan, who'd stated that it seemed pretty clear that Haldane was judging everything in relationship to his own experience. Just leave yourself open to possibilities, he'd suggested. This could not only be *fun*—but it could result in better relationships all around.

Haldane was also uneasy about Podly's enthusiasm, he thought, as their vehicle tilted down toward a flat clearing. It just wasn't like the captain to up and skedaddle right in the middle of a serious murder investigation. Of course, Brogan was likely right—the assassin was probably an Earth man imported for the hit, a professional who most likely had the smarts not to try another one, just get out of town. Still, skipping out of town while that business guy's blood was still wet on the sidewalk wasn't like Podly. It wasn't as if the captain didn't deserve a vacation—he most certainly did. It just wasn't in his character to be so frenzied and enthusiastic.

Also, he was a little worried about Brogan.

His partner seemed bothered about something. It was as though someone had trodden over his grave. Something about that crime scene they'd scoped out had bothered him. Something about that rock he'd picked up . . .

Brogan had carried it around with him everywhere, and had scheduled the thing to be analyzed in the police labs.

But then he'd lost it.

That had seemed to bother Brogan the most. Although Haldane hadn't thought it was even related, and emphasized that to his partner, Brogan was clearly vexed by the disappearance, and the possibility that it could be something that might lead them to the identity of the killer.

Where could it have gone?

Disappeared into thin air?

The problem with being on an alien planet like Altor was that you never really knew if maybe that couldn't very possibly be just the case.

Haldane peered down at the island.

Just what went *on* down there, anyway?

"There it is!" called Podly, pointing down and off to the right. "The compound. Gentlepeople, I promise you that some meaningful experiences await you down there!"

Haldane looked mournfully over to Brogan. Brogan shrugged and then said, "We're all set for whatever, Captain. *Now* can you give us a more concrete hint about what we can expect?"

Podly leaned back and grinned. This alarmed Haldane greatly. Podly smiling was bad enough. But *grinning*? It wasn't a pretty sight. Haldane ardently hoped he didn't make a habit of it.

"Just let the experience take you in its jaws and thrash you around a bit. Foreshadowing will spoil the impact," said the Creon.

"I'm not entirely sure I'm comforted by your figures of speech, sir," said Brogan.

"Yeah, Captain Podly. We're not going to be in danger here, are we?" said Haldane.

"Of course not. But what would life be without a little element of risk, right?" The pilot chose that moment to veer sharply downward, causing a lurch. "Hey! What are you trying to do," called Podly to the pilot, "kill us?"

"No sir."

"Well, have a care! I don't want my friends to die before the good part comes."

Haldane blanched. "Actually, neither do we."

Danger in the line of duty was one thing.

Danger in the line of police relations was another. Time would tell how far they'd have to go with this business, and what exactly they'd have to do. However, all in all, Jack Haldane would rather be in Philadelphia . . . preferably with a good-looking woman.

"Interesting architecture," said Brogan.

Haldane thought it was interesting as well, as far as that went. He didn't know from architecture. This collection looked vaguely alien, sort of like something from a twentieth century B sci-fi movie. Or, more precisely, like a collection of building blocks. Domes and spokes and protrusions. He just hoped they had hot water and indoor plumbing. The clump of buildings was surrounded on all sides by walls. Beyond were patterns of partially regimented wilderness. Trees and plains. Lakes, lagoons, sea, and mountains.

"The architecture?" said Podly. "Well, thank you, I suppose, but we just put it all together on the cheap, and we add on when we can. I should hasten to point out here that this island isn't only ours. There are other Creon and Tarn male societies on Demeter City." He shook his head mournfully. "No, we police couldn't afford a whole island on *our* salaries."

"Ah. Kind of like time-sharing vacations on the Jersey Shore," said Haldane helpfully.

"Time-sharing. Yes, that would seem to be an appropriate term," said Podly.

The cruiser settled down on the paved landing field. Haldane waited for the safety precautions to click into operation, and then he unlatched his belt array and looked out to see what was up.

Standing on the edge of the tarmac was a waiting assembly of Creons and Tarns, all dressed in the best official police uniforms, the equivalent of Napoleonic military finery. There were epaulets in abundance, lace and fluff at necks and cuffs, and huge colorful hats covered with enough feathers to power a flock of birds.

Drums began to pound. Alien equivalents to trumpets tooted. A baton waved in the hand of one particularly brightly plumed martinet, and some kind of martial anthem piped up, sounding like John Philip Sousa vomiting violas to groaning brass accompaniment.

The grin on Podly's face somehow grew larger. "Beautiful, yes? Don't you just love pageantry."

The pilot hopped out and opened the doors for them. As Haldane stepped out onto the landing field, the marching band of Creons and Tarns commenced to parade toward them.

Boom boom boom, went a ball-shaped drum, as a pair of young Creons, clearly of rookie status, pounded their heads into it.

Toot toot toot, sounded the hornlike instruments, more like whoopee cushions than their earthly equivalent.

Squawk squawk squawk, belted an array of

instruments unlike anything in Haldane's experience: big bags with keys and nozzles. The nearest thing on Earth, he supposed, would be bagpipes, only these things made bagpipes sound like chorused sweet heavenly melodies.

"Is this the normal welcome for newcomers?" asked Brogan, clearly slightly nonplussed by the whole display.

"I thought," explained Podly, "that since you are the first human males to be inducted into our membership, we should put on a particularly sublime and elegant display of our artistic natures. If it were just me, they would have just brought out the squeak-bags and played a little token ditty."

Haldane and Brogan exchanged looks.

"Well, we sure are honored," said Haldane.

"Pah!" said Podly dismissively. "Wait until we bring out the chorus and windsack orchestra for the closing ceremonies. You will depart Dreek Island with nothing short of awe, I promise."

Just short of the big cruiser, the parade stopped.

A Creon wearing a hat that made him look like Lord Nelson under a grow light stepped out, holding a scroll.

"Quite the ceremony," said Brogan.

"Only the best for my good friends," said Podly.

He made a deep bow to the new arrival.

The new arrival bowed back, then let go of the bottom of the scroll. It unraveled and thunked onto the tarmac.

"Greetings, greetings, greetings!" sang out the Creon, shaking his head back and forth in a practiced motion that could only be a signal for ceremony, yet looked for all the galaxy like some sort of backseat car ornament after hitting a couple of bumps. "Welcome, O citizens of another planet. Your glandular secretions become you. All hail the glories of maleness. Let us lock our organs together in a spirited ejaculation, spreading seeds of inspiration for the entire Universe."

"Oh my God," gasped Haldane. Uncomfortably literal visions sprouted in his head.

Podly chuckled. "Oh, don't worry. He speaks purely in metaphorical terms."

"Those guys are not going to get anywhere near *my* metaphors!" said Haldane.

"Hey, loosen up, guy," whispered Brogan. "We're on an alien planet. This isn't Earth."

"No kidding, Sherlock!"

"Just observe the proceedings, take part only as much as you care to—and remember, smile!"

Haldane hoisted the sides of his mouth up as well as he could manage and showed his state of pleased approval to the assembled Tarns and Creons bashing and blowing at their instruments. Alerted to the meaning of this human expression, the welcoming band felt appropriately validated. They rewarded the visitors with yet more energy and enthusiasm. Several hopped up and down. One rolled upon the ground, pleasing Podly no end.

"Oh my," he said, gripping his hands together and shaking them before his fellows, shouting above this din. "A truly magnificent performance, Brethren! I'm sure our new human guests feel very welcomed."

"We do indeed," said Brogan, imitating the gesture.

"Uhmm—oh, yes, certainly," said Haldane, locking hands and following suit. By now the smell of their greeters—a curious combination of flowery and earth scents, with a touch of what might have been beer—had wafted his way, tickling his nostrils.

At that moment, a car about the size of a golf cart zoomed up from the service building, stopping in front of the celebrants.

A large Creon with a scar running down the side of his face got out, pushing a frown toward them.

Podly's smile wilted.

Jack Haldane was no psychic, but he could feel the hackles of his neck rise up.

He'd seen this guy before. And he was giving off worse vibes than ever.

But then maybe he was misinterpreting. He'd seen plenty of dangerous-looking aliens that had turned out mild as milk. And some aliens who seemed meek that were dangerous.

"Greetings, Cradla," said Podly. "I was not aware that you would be joining in these festivities."

"Podly," said the Creon with a taste of menace in his voice, bushy eyebrows rising high. "I would not miss the induction of humans into our joyous assembly for worlds."

CHAPTER

They had planned
their arrival at Dreek Island for after sundown,
and their navigation and sense of timing had been
impeccable. Just as the last rays of the sun were
slipping over the horizon and stars were fading in
the nighttime sky, Jane Castle got a sensor fix on
the place.

"There it is," she called up from her position in
the navigation chair. She read off the coordinates.
Immediately, Took made adjustments in the pilot
program and prepared for when she would take
over on manual. "Dreek Island."

"Looks most curious," said Ted Bickford, in the
backseat. "Forbidding, even."

He took out a gun, cocked it loudly.

The sound made Jane jump.

"What are you doing, Ted?" she asked.

"Checking out weapons systems."

Settled back nonchalantly in the depths of the backseat, he said it in a light, jokey voice, in the same tone as if he were commenting on the weather or talking about a pleasant past experience—or a much-anticipated future one.

Took had been a bit taken aback that Jane had enlisted help for this venture. It all sounded good in theory, but in actuality, it was clear when they met that Took was not exactly smitten by Ted. Maybe his slick good looks or aplomb hit her the wrong way. Who knew. In any event, Took had taken her aside later on, after the initial planning session.

"I don't know about that guy," she said, sipping at a cup of *maka* tea, worry lines wrapped around the third eye of her forehead.

"What's not to know?"

"What *do* you know about him anyway, Jane?"

"I told you. We can trust him."

"Why do you say that? Because he used to be a boyfriend?" Took said doubtfully.

"He's a freelance engineer, as I said. He's okay. He'll be able to help us, as I mentioned. What's wrong, Took? Red Alert on the psychic channel? If so, I need to know."

"Not exactly."

"What's wrong then?"

Took pursed her lips. "I don't know. It's not psychic exactly. In fact, I'm getting positive psychic readings from him."

"So what's wrong with that."

"They're *too* positive."

"Okay. So you're saying that I chose the right person to help us, a person who can be trusted and who, as I mentioned, believes emphatically in our cause."

"I mean, it's not . . . well, natural. Everybody's a mix. It's like he's controlling it. I get no inkling of the darker parts of him."

"Okay, okay, that doesn't mean they're not there. Couldn't this just be a faulty chip in that impressive woo-woo array there in that pretty skull?"

"Maybe."

"I think it is." Jane had laughed. "Look, as I say, Tookie. He likes me."

"Yes, I can sense that."

"He didn't write after our little . . . uhm . . . affaire de coeur . . . He feels bad about it. That's one of the reasons he wants to go with us. He wants to make that gaffe up to me. What could be more natural?"

"Has that little coeur thing resumed?"

"What? After not writing? Of course not . . . Not yet, anyway." A knowing smile had spread over Jane's smooth features.

"Not until he helps you with this."

"Precisely . . . If then . . ."

"So you're saying you trust him because you think he's doing this to get back into your affections . . . And your arms."

"With men, Took, you need but examine the passions that drive them. Passions they may not be totally aware of, passions they may rationalize—but passions nonetheless."

"So—you think that you're manipulating him?" Jane was incensed. "Nothing of the kind!"

"I don't know, Jane. Sounds like the old-fashioned womanly wiles. I thought you were above that."

"I deny everything, Took. I deny those accusations emphatically!" She smiled. "However, I will admit to two minor sins. First, the extreme desire to expose the chauvinistic shenanigans of the controlling male pigs of the police force."

"Strong language."

"Maybe. Let me finish. Second, to be perfectly honest, I guess I still have a soft spot in my heart for Ted. Confession time and all that. So I'm a little hard to get . . . Makes him work harder. I get help, he gets eventual . . . affection. We get each other, for whatever time we have." She held up hands in surrender to calculated fate. "Everybody wins."

"Except the other males."

"They deserve to be taken down a peg, don't you think?"

Took sighed. "Perhaps. Nonetheless, I'll warn you now, I don't feel entirely good about this."

"Oh, Took. Just think of it as a grand adventure in the cause of our sex."

"And you believe that this Ted Bickford believes that."

Jane Castle raised her eyebrows. "Perhaps not quite in that word order."

So, Jane knew that Took wasn't totally thrilled with Ted's company. And now, she wasn't totally thrilled with the way he was playing with his gun. He'd insisted on bringing one. He said he'd have no trouble in getting a permit, and he didn't. (It wouldn't do, after all, to bring an illegal gun onto an island full of police officers.) However, she had to agree to the wisdom of carrying defensive measures.

After all, if they were going to be skulking about in the wild where creatures were hunted— well, then, those creatures were most certainly dangerous.

Still, he didn't have to be so noisy and obvious with his gun. She had one, and it was safely tucked to one side, ready if needed, but hardly something that preoccupied her. Just where a good police-person's gun should be.

"And, pray tell," she said, turning back to look at his dim form in the backseat, "just how are those weapons systems?"

"A little scary, frankly. I'm afraid an engineer doesn't get to use guns much." Voice still light and friendly. "As I said, I've shot in galleries and ranges—and VirtSims. Never gone hunting before, though. Sheesh. I sure hope I don't actually have to *use* this thing."

"Maybe you'd better put it back in your pack then," said Took, softly but emphatically. "Your inexperience is making me a little uncomfortable."

"Sure. Hate to make my companions in adventure nervous—Hell, I'm nervous enough as it is." He laughed. "An island of cops with much bigger guns than these—guy cops, yet, on an island where females aren't allowed. I'm colluding with the distaff enemy. Now *that's* nervous making."

"I believe we're competent enough to execute my

plans here," said Jane, staring down and concentrating on her equipment. Wouldn't do to land in the water—and there was plenty of that hereabouts to land in, that was for sure.

"I just hope your plans are all that get executed," said Ted. He made a show of putting away his handgun. "Speaking of weapons, have you got the rest of yours?"

Jane smiled. "Are you speaking in a journalistic sense, Mr. Bickford?"

"I am, oh able undercover reporter."

"Yes. I've got top tech cameras, taping devices, and long-range adjustments for them both. I have tapping devices and bugs. Indeed, I have the best of what our dear precinct has to offer."

"How did you manage that, Jane?" said Took.

"Tohnor down in Requisitions. Beyond the fact that she *owes* me," said Jane blithely, "I told her what's afoot. Tohnor is all for what we're doing. She would have loved to come—only the force is down to bare bones because of this Dreek Island thing this week."

Took tsk-tsked. "Yes, and with an assassin loose."

That seemed to attract Ted's interest. He leaned over the seat, draping his now-empty hands onto the plast-sheen cushion rests. "Yeah," he said. "Boy, I heard about that. Nasty business, huh? Hope you guys get a hold of who's responsible."

"We're not doing our best, I'm afraid," said Jane. "Not with the males cavorting on this island of shame."

"Oh, reporter, it sounds as though we're venturing into the language of sensationalistic and quite, quite yellow journalism," said Ted in an admonishing tone.

"I don't care where or how it's printed . . . Just as long as we get proof about this sorry business," said Jane. "Proof that we can use to change this unjust practice."

They were all wearing what amounted to what Ted had earlier dubbed "commando gear": camouflage khakis and dark work boots. Knapsacks supplied space for what they needed to carry, including food and a tent, if for some reason they would not be able to sleep tonight in the hopper. Also, Jane had included water containers, and blackening for the face in case they had to crawl through vegetation or whatnot. Fire-starting equipment, knives: full survival gear. She'd not only had plenty of training in this regard: this kind of roughing it was a form of recreation for her and had been since she was a girl. Jane had four older brothers, roughnecks the lot. She knew her way around things traditionally reserved for males, and she'd received plenty of respect not just from those brothers, but from all the males back in Europe. This was one of the several reasons why all of this inequality here on the Demeter City Police Force was so galling.

Jane quickly reported the sensor numeral output.

"Okay. We're going down," said Took, tapping in the coordinates that Jane had given her.

"We heading in low to avoid radar?" asked Ted.

"I checked. No radar here on Dreek Island. Why should there be? There aren't any nations or armed conflict here in that sense," said Jane. "It's not like we're on Earth."

"Pardon?" said Took, not taking her eyes off the controls, bringing them down in a smooth descent toward the island.

"Little hobby of Earth nations," said Bickford in a sardonic tone. "Attacking one another."

"Yes. I'm afraid even in this stellar age," Jane agreed, "we have not yet gotten out of the war habit."

"War is nothing new in the galaxy," said Took. "It is fortunate indeed that Tarns and Creons do not war—we are such different peoples. In fact, that brings up a point I wished to make about this whole business. I just wanted to say—"

The hopper was buffeted. The wheel shuddered, whipping out of Took's hands. The hopper veered, canted, started a downward dive.

"What's going on?" cried Jane.

"Some kind of wind shear," returned Took, fighting the controls.

"Damn," said Bickford. "And me without my seat belt on!"

Another jolt, and the engineer was flung over the seat.

"Took. Do something!"

Took was busy jabbing controls. Bickford twisted around, groaned, reached out a hand, and pulled a lever.

Immediately the hopper righted itself, steadied.

The man pulled himself back over the front seat, plopped back, and let out a loud sigh. "Wow! Let's hope that's the extent of excitement on this trip."

Took rapidly gained control, and continued downward.

Jane recovered her aplomb. "How did you know to do that, Ted?"

"Hmmm? Oh, I've had a little training in this kind of vehicle before. They have something very similar back on Earth, you know."

"No. I didn't know." She dismissed the whole thing. "Thanks. That seldom happens."

"Thanks indeed. I'm afraid I'm not a first-class hopper driver. Maybe I should have been navigating."

"Don't worry, you all are doing just fine. It's lucky I remember my instructor pointing out just this kind of situation and what to do about it."

Jane was vaguely annoyed and vaguely upset, and she wasn't quite sure why. But she shrugged it off and concentrated on the looming mass of land rising up before them.

"Down there," said Took. "That must be the compound."

Jane peered down.

Amid the dark of vegetation and rock, there were forms of buildings exuding light and a bulky presence. She could make out no moving signs of life, but still better, nothing to alert the males below that another vessel was soon to be landing on Dreek Island.

"Took. Better take it down around the other side

of that hill over there. That looks like a safe place to park this thing."

"Right," said Took, and they went down.

There were no sentries.

The wall itself around the perimeter of the compound was not at all difficult to scale.

Within a very short time of landing, the interlopers on Dreek Island were over that wall and creeping up to what looked to be the main meeting hall.

Jane Castle led them. It was pretty obvious that something significant was going on here. Light and music and loud noises were spilling out through open windows.

"You've got your equipment?" said Bickford.

"You bet," said Jane, displaying her devices.

Took said, "Let's do this and get out of here."

Jane said nothing. She didn't want her friend to know that what she had in mind was going to take longer than just an in-and-out jaunt.

Odd, spirited, off-key music issued from the building. It sounded like an oompah band on bad drugs. The closer they got to the building, the more it seemed to thump and shake. There was the smell of roasting meat and less savory things exuding from the structure.

The whole scene had the definite taste of excess.

Perfect.

Carefully, making sure they stayed in the shadows, they made their way up the landing and peered cautiously into the window.

"Hmm," whispered Bickford. "This is quite something!"

"Oh my!" said Took.

After she got over her shock and surprise, Jane realized that she'd better start recording.

She pulled up her devices and hit the appropriate buttons, grinning to herself.

Dear me, she thought. This display the guys were putting on was far more outrageous than she could ever have possibly imagined!

Cradla.

Patrick Brogan had met the Creon before, briefly. He worked at another administrative office. Frankly, though, even allowing for interspecies differences, Brogan had never liked the guy.

Subcaptain Cradla.

Now that they were on this island, in this situation, he would just have to make the best of it, and now, as he held out his hand in greeting to the just-arrived Creon on the airstrip, he smiled casually.

"It's a great honor to be welcomed into your fraternity. We just hope we're worthy of the honor," he said.

"Yeah!" said Haldane, holding out his hand as well.

Cradla looked down at the extended hands, curling

his lip with contempt. "We do not accept Earth customs here, gentle beings."

Podly looked uncomfortable. "Oh Cradla. Get off your high *marma* quadruped! Shake our human friends' hands."

Still smiling, Brogan dropped his hand. Haldane did the same. "That's not necessary."

"Our mistake."

"We're quite happy to observe the local customs."

Cradla nodded. "You are wise to. We are an august and old organization and take our traditions very, very seriously."

"Perhaps, Cradla," said Podly, "it's necessary to illustrate the Dreek Island Fraternity greeting."

"I would have wished you had better educated your nominated inductees earlier," said the Creon, with a thoughtful sigh. "Oh very well."

He was smaller than Podly, with a sleeker, better-shaped head. And though his body was more compact, it was better shaped, more muscular, and obviously better conditioned. Cradla had a prissy, picky air about him, and he smelled overmuch of the popular Creon cologne. His uniform was sharply creased and perfectly tailored. Brogan wasn't crazy about this aspect of the creature; but there was something else that bothered him. He couldn't quite put his finger on it, though.

By the look on Haldane's face—as though he were sucking on a particularly sour candy—Brogan could see he felt pretty much the same way.

It was well-known around the precinct that

Cradla resented Podly for being promoted over him into the position of captain of the Main Space Precinct, and felt generally underappreciated. Oddly enough, Podly took all this very magnanimously, and seemed absolutely cordial to his peer. So far, there'd been no underhanded office politics on either side as far as Brogan knew. However, Cradla had complained to those in charge a number of times, and that news had filtered down to the ranks, many of whom considered the choice a matter of choosing between the Devil and the Deep Blue Sea.

As much as he found Podly's temper and austerity hard to deal with sometimes, Brogan was squarely on his captain's side. There was something oily, nasty, and dishonest there in Cradla, beneath that oily, nasty, and dissembling exterior.

A hush swept over the assembly as the two captains stepped up to each other.

For one moment, they stood nose to nose.

Then they turned.

"I greet you, Brother," said Cradla, looking as though he were pulling his own teeth with the words.

"I greet you with respect, Brother," said Podly.

The two turned, and bumped their buttocks together three times.

Brogan's jaw felt like it was threatening to dust off the ground. Beside him, Haldane had to stop himself from giggling aloud.

The assemblage exploded with cheers.

Podly stepped away. "Now. Would you gentleman care to try our greeting with Cradla?"

"Ah—my posterior needs rest," said Cradla. "May I beg off for the time being, with promises for a truly fine greeting, say, tomorrow? However, if you insist on greetings . . . well, then, allow Axla to be my proxy."

The Creon waved a hand blithely.

From out of the crowd a huge Creon emerged. His bright-colored uniform was too small for him. It stretched at the buttons and the breeches. His face was the size of a giant watermelon, and he had hands like hams. The eyes looked a little dull, and he exuded the smell of dumb muscle.

"Axla. Axla, greet our new prospective member," said Cradla.

"I greet you, Brothers," said Axla.

"You first, partner," said Haldane. "Take some of the vinegar out of him."

With a doubtful expression, Brogan stepped forward to face the Creon. Axla duly turned around. Brogan turned as well. He pushed his posterior out to meet Axla's.

The next thing he knew, he was kissing hard concrete.

Cheering from the assembled grew, and the band struck up again.

Brogan got up and brushed himself off, trying to keep his aplomb and maintain the smile on his face.

"Next," grunted Axla.

Brogan turned a pained look to his partner. "That would be you, I believe, Jack."

"Yeah. I'm afraid so."

Jack's eyes seemed planted on the enormous

posterior that awaited him. *Rather sumo wrestler-ish,* thought Brogan.

He was happy to see that he'd lost no dignity in the encounter—except, perhaps, in his own mind.

Jack Haldane stepped up.

"I greet you, Brother," he said.

"I greet *you*, Brother," said Axla.

They turned around and bumped.

Haldane, despite his determined effort to give as good as he got, hurtled past Brogan, tumbling onto the hard field.

The greeters cheered.

Brogan stepped over and helped him up.

"You okay, buddy?"

"Oh yeah. Tubby there looks a lot happier than we are, though." He looked around. "We're not on 'Candid Camera,' are we?"

"We should be so lucky," replied Brogan.

"Well then. You're good sports," said Podly. "You showed old Cradla what your mettle is."

"Wish our mettle was a little more metallic," said Haldane, rubbing his rump.

"Come this way. Food and drink and surprises await at the compound!"

"Uhm, Captain," said Brogan. "Could we take the food and drink and hold the surprises?"

Podly bellowed with laughter. "Ha! A very good one. No, I think you two will do very well indeed on Dreek Island."

Brogan looked at Haldane, and Haldane returned the exact same resigned look.

They walked over to the waiting vehicles.

The gates of the compound were open.

It really was a rather nice-looking place, weird alien architecture notwithstanding, thought Brogan. The trees and flowers were especially luxuriant and abundant, spreading tastefully about the place in tendrils and clumps. The place somehow managed to affect the look of both old and new. From all that Brogan had heard, this men's assembly had been in place from the moment that the Creons had landed from their home planet of Danae. Tarns were inducted later.

As he walked into the courtyard and received blasts of scent and the sensation of established order and pride, Brogan had a slightly different opinion about this organization. However bizarre or just odd it was, it had value for some reason to the participants. How and why was something that, hopefully, they would eventually learn.

"I presume you heard about Maelish," said Cradla, as they walked along to what looked to be the main building.

"Yes. I was deeply saddened by the news," said Podly.

"He was hunting *zark*. The *zark* got him, alas." Cradla turned to the island's new guests. "Be forewarned. Most of this island is a wild, wild place. And very dangerous."

"Warning taken," said Haldane. "I'll just stay inside and read a book."

The notion of Haldane's actually reading a book for pleasure was strange enough, but the idea of going to a dangerous island for fun was slightly appalling to Brogan. Didn't these guys get enough action in the streets of Demeter City? *He* certainly did.

"I hadn't heard about this. You usually hear when a cop gets killed," said Brogan.

Podly shook his head mournfully. "This sort of death we don't publicize. We'd have to tell the public at large about the island, and, as this is a secret society, that is strictly forbidden."

"Wait a minute," said Haldane. "If most of the professional Creon males of Demeter City know about this place—what's the secret?"

"A secret," intoned Cradla imperiously, "is a secret when it is called a secret. Until," he continued, in a breathier, sharper tone, "it is not."

That sounded suitably abstruse and alien to Brogan. He shot a look to his partner: give it a rest. From time to time they tended to pay attention to the similarities between humans and other-worlders. Now it was time to respect the dissimilarities. Haldane seemed to get the message. He shut up.

"How true," said Podly, thoughtfully. The clouds upon his face suddenly lifted. He clapped his hands together, and spread his arms. "But we can't dwell on yesterday's misfortunes too long. I suspect we'll have a memorial or something for old Maelish and bang a few *dak* sticks to send him off in style. But for now, we should be sure to make our new *human* members welcome."

"Welcome!" cried the chorus of other Tarns and

Creons. A festive mood suddenly prevailed again, despite Cradla's continued scowl.

"You know, I don't *like* that guy very much," whispered Haldane to Brogan.

"What's to like."

"He's definitely the turd in the punch bowl."

"We'll drink around him."

"Yes, absolutely," said Podly. "And now, we will show our new friends to their quarters!"

They were led to a building with living accommodations that seemed spartan but perfectly adequate. They had their own private bathroom. They had some time to themselves, and so they cleaned up. Tonight was to be a feast and a special ceremony of some kind.

"Relax. Have a nap. Stroll around the library downstairs if you like. Watch a vid," Podly had said. "But by all means don't exert yourself. We stay up very late at night. And I promise, a good time will be had by all!"

While Haldane was sudsing up in the shower, Brogan took a stroll in the lobby. Looked like a regular, if bucolic, camp hotel lobby to him, with chairs and shelves of books, games, and the promised vids. Brogan selected a couple of magazines and was just about to return to the room when something smacked him lightly in the back of the head.

He turned around swiftly, just in time to see something flutter to the floor. There was no sign of anyone in the lobby. He looked down and saw that he'd been struck in the back of the head with a paper airplane.

He picked it up and opened it.

In cut-out, block letters the thing read: BEWARE.

In English, yet. Lovely. Brogan folded the paper and put it in his back pocket.

Then he had a thought. Was this a true threat? Was there something happening on this island that could cause him and Haldane harm?

Or was this all part of the initiation, some kind of trick?

It had that melodramatic touch to it. Brogan hadn't seen this kind of message in a long time. It was something out of a lame old movie!

He took the magazines back to the room.

Haldane was stretched on the bed. There was a cartoon on the vid—the Creon equivalent of Mickey Mouse. The kids watched it, even though they thought it was highly weird; maybe because of that. Haldane, though, seemed not merely to comprehend it, but to be totally engrossed.

Brogan pulled out the note. "What do you make of this?" he said, handing it to his partner.

"Where'd you get this?" asked Haldane.

"Downstairs. Hit me in the back of the head in paper airplane form."

"Well, on first glance I'd say it's stage two of haze the Earth people. That doesn't mean that we shouldn't be careful."

"Yeah. That's my opinion."

"Can't fault them for entertainment," said Haldane. "Looks like we might actually have a good time."

"Are you having a good time now?"

"Starting to."

"We'll see. I can't help but feel trepidation."

"Just be ready for anything."

There was a knock on the door. Brogan went over and opened it. Standing there was a tall Tarn holding clothing wrapped in plastic.

"Your evening attire, sirs, fitted exactly to your measurements."

The Tarn held out two elegant ladies' ballroom gowns—one pink, the other a soft mauve.

"And your makeup."

With his other hand he held out a box.

Brogan looked back at Haldane.

"True," said Haldane. "I wasn't expecting *this*."

CHAPTER

"Excellent," said Podly
"You look *most* appropriate."

"Thank you," said Patrick Brogan, feeling ambivalent about the whole situation.

"You look especially fetching, Officer Haldane."

"Wish I could say I felt that way," said Jack Haldane, nervously peering about the hall, as though checking to make sure there wasn't anyone here important to him who would see him like this.

Brogan couldn't blame him. He just hoped against hope that nobody was taking pictures of this thing tonight.

"Smile!" cried a short Tarn.

A flashstrobe went off in Brogan's face, leaving him blinking.

Oh well. So much for that.

The sun had set.

They had been summoned for supper and the special ceremony in the main meeting hall. It had taken all of Brogan's powers of persuasion to get Haldane into his gown. No, he assured his partner—he had absolutely *no idea* why this was necessary, but it was part of the deal. In for a dime, in for a dollar. Besides, this was supposed to be fun. What, Brogan had asked patiently, could be more fun than dressing up in fancy ballroom gowns for a bunch of aliens?

How about a jab in the eye with a sharp stick, Haldane had suggested morosely.

The makeup had almost been the undoing of the whole arrangement. Lipstick, rouge, eye shadow, eyeliner—all of which neither Brogan nor Haldane knew a thing about applying.

In the midst of this crisis, they'd received a call from Podly. "How's it going, my good friends!"

"Uhm—why exactly do you want us to wear *dresses*, sir?"

"This is custom. To dress up as females. It has deep psychological meaning—and besides, it makes for a good guffaw or two."

"Yes, I can imagine that."

"Don't be concerned for your dignity," said Podly. "We shall all be wearing dresses and other accoutrements of the females of our races. Does that make you feel better, then, friend?"

"Er—sure, I suppose so. You want to talk to Haldane, though."

"No need, Lieutenant. Tell him it's an *order*. See you soon for the fest!"

The phone clicked off with finality.

Haldane sighed, got up, and took the plastic off his gown.

Now, as they entered the meeting hall, Brogan realized that Podly was right. He didn't feel as strange.

Everybody looked odd, to say the least.

And while he and Jack looked absolutely ludicrous in dresses and makeup (actually, Jack looked rather pretty, though he'd never think of telling him that), the others looked just plain bizarre.

At least he and Jack were dressed tastefully. The other costumes looked absolutely garish. At least the Creon outfits did . . . the Tarn costumes seemed more appealing, like colorful togas sprigged with flowers.

The Creons, though, looked like Carmen Miranda imitations on LSD.

"What do you think?" said Podly, his fruit-hat wobbling uncertainly atop his big head. The captain performed a pirouette, the colorful oddments hanging from his floor-length dress twirling happily.

"Stunning, sir," said Jack Haldane.

"Very nice!" said Brogan. "Although, truth to tell, I think that you look more at home in your uniform."

Podly had a large wooden container that smelled of *darkan* brew. His eyes glittered with uncharacteristic good humor. "Of course! But every once in a while, every Creon—begorrah! every living thing has to let loose and *party!*"

"Hey, can I have some of that drink?" asked Haldane. "I usually keep away from the stuff, but I think I'll make tonight an exception."

"Of course!" The Creon captain raised his fingers and snapped them.

Immediately, waiters rushed forward carrying huge containers of the yeasty stuff. Haldane grabbed one gratefully and took a large gulp, but Brogan demurred.

"Not now, I think."

"Oh, get into the *spirit*," said Podly. "So to speak."

To please his boss, Brogan took one of the containers. Had a small sip. He'd nurse it, that was all—he felt the need to keep his wits about him, after that note. True, it could have been just a part of this induction. But if it wasn't, there had to be at least one sober judgment in human attendance.

"Yow!" said Haldane. "This is *strong*."

"A special vintage. The brewmaster made this vat especially for tonight," said Cradla dryly. He wore a slightly more tasteful baggy assemblage of colors than Podly, and in fact looked a great deal more adept in carrying off his particular masquerade. He sipped at his own cup thoughtfully. "Quite amusing apparel, gentlepeople. It actually makes me happy to see you here. I don't doubt your good humor and cooperation now will go a long way in easing your way into the acceptance of our comrades here."

"That's good to know," said Brogan. "Because most certainly that is the way we would wish it."

"I hate to ask what's next," said Haldane. He brought the cup down from his face and a ring of foam lined his upper lip "But—what's next?"

The true question is, thought Brogan, *do we really want to know.*

"Nothing out of the ordinary, m'boy," said Podly. "We eat, we drink, we celebrate the joy of being males!" The Creon took another hefty swallow of *darkan*.

"In female apparel?" Haldane looked baffled. Brogan just wished he would shut up and take this whole thing like a man . . . or rather, like a man dressed in an evening gown.

Cradla took a demure sip from his own drinking vessel and surveyed the assemblage coolly through his dark, unreadable eyes. "Are you requesting the rationale here—or the psychology?" he asked blithely.

"Either will do, I guess."

"Creon psychology—well that's a whole can of worms I hesitate to open for outsiders." Cradla touched at a mottled ear thoughtfully. "But since you are worthy of the formidable Captain Podly's trust and respect, we should perhaps clue you in."

Haldane suddenly looked as though he was wondering if he really cared to know. But Brogan's interest picked up. In fact, every little scrap of knowledge would be helpful here, in understanding xenopsychology.

"It's very simple, really," said Cradla. "There are strong lines drawn between males and females of the Creon race. Each individual has particular roles he or she must perform according to strict and regimented rules. Any sign of femininity on the part of males is strongly frowned upon, and signs of masculinity in females are equally discouraged. Naturally, as in any species, there are elements of both sexes in each individual. This male Creon rite—which Tarns took to quite readily, I might add—allows a time apart from females in which individuals can revel in certain aspects of the female character, symbolized in their clothing."

"We call it cross-dressing back home on Earth," said Haldane. "And boy, if the guys on my New York force saw me in one of these, I'd never live it down."

"It sounds as though your people could use one evening a year of similar foolishness," sniffed Cradla. "Very good for the soul, I assure you."

"Great. I'll save on therapy sessions later," said Haldane.

Brogan looked around. The hall was filled with long tables by which chairs sat patiently. Plates and cutlery of various colorful patterns sat neatly upon the tables, and there were centerpieces of exotic and sweet-smelling flowers. "You mentioned dinner. But I don't see anything . . . and come to think of it, I don't smell anything cooking."

"Over there," said Podly, pointing.

A group of Creons stood around a huge cooking pot, above which tendrils of steam were just beginning to creep. They wore aprons and funny-shaped chefs' hats.

Haldane stepped over, peered.

"Hey Captain Podly. Looks like just plain old boiling water," he said, his look of bafflement still serving him well.

"No. It's Catch Stew. Stage one," replied Podly.

He bellowed. "Let's get on to some chow!"

The others yelled back their approval of this notion loudly.

Doors swung open. A large box was rolled out to the center of the room. Looks of eagerness and excitement filled many a Creon and Tarn eye.

Two chests were rolled out after them. The lids were opened and a group huddled around them while three chunky Creons heaved the box open.

A huge mass of Altorian rats, snakes, insects, and other creatures of the scurrying variety were dumped upon the floor. They began to scuttle, creep, and slither in various directions.

The group began pulling out mallets from the chests, and hurriedly passing them around.

Podly thrust one into Brogan's hand.

"As I said, m'boy," he announced, charging into the fray, "a most excellent dish. Catch Stew!"

"I think," said Haldane, staring at his own weapon, "I've lost my appetite."

The preparation of the first course of Catch Stew was a somewhat messy and frantic affair, but all the Creons present seemed to enjoy it immensely.

Both he and Haldane were given full bowls of the stuff. Creon cooking had never been Patrick Brogan's favorite part of his move to Demeter City, and looking down at the mangled pieces of dead creatures in this bowl was doing absolutely nothing to change his mind.

He looked over at Haldane, who sat, hovering over his bowl, holding his spoon, and looking absolutely miserable.

Meanwhile, the rest of the assembly were slurping and chomping away happily, washing down this first course with great swallows of brew. This dribbled down the chins and bibs of the Creons, often spilling onto their dresses. What surprised Brogan was that the Tarns were only slightly more fastidious. In fact, the usually reserved and thoughtful Tarns were indulging in this feast with astonishing gusto and joy.

Brogan looked down at his stew.

A tentacle flopped forlornly over the rim of the bowl. The scent that rose from the congealed, oozing mass was something a good deal less than savory.

He lifted the spoon.

There was a floating eyeball staring up at him. He let the spoon drop back and turned to Haldane.

"Any suggestions?"

"Yeah. Let's not eat this."

"We're the special guests. We'll offend them."

"It's that or offend our digestive systems." Haldane's bowl had been teetering on the edge of the table. A nudge of the spoon sent it spinning over and flopping onto the floor, splattering stew.

The gorging assembly barely seemed to notice.

"Oops."

Not particularly happy about taking that course,

Brogan instead picked his bowl up. "I think I'll just
go get a breath of fresh air for a moment!" he said.
And fertilize the bushes while I'm at it.

Just at the door, he ran into Captain Podly.

"How are you enjoying your stew, then,
Patrick?"

"Ummm . . . absolutely delicious."

"And look . . . You've got yourself a real delicacy
in there. May I?"

"Certainly."

Podly reached in with his thick fingers and
pulled out a long, snaky thing.

"Musk lizard tail. You lucky fellow."

"You know, if you like them—Why then go
ahead and take it."

Podly smiled. "Oh, I couldn't think of it. But it
would do my Creon heart"—he placed a broad hand
on his stomach—"so much good to see you enjoy it,
Patrick."

"Uhmmm . . . uhmm . . . I'm afraid that we humans
can't really deal with long sinuous things like that.
We choke, you know."

"Well, chew it up good. You'll get more flavor
that way."

He was on the spot. There was nothing else for
Brogan to do but to take the cooked tail and put it
in his mouth.

It was like gristly spaghetti.

He chewed as much as he dared and then gulped
the thing down, trying not to make too much noise.

"Damned tasty, eh?" said Podly, patting his pro-
tégé on the back.

Brogan coughed in response and forced himself to smile. "Yummy."

His stomach gurgled in rebellion.

Podly bellied his way back up to the *darkan* keg, allowing Brogan to make his way outside. Looking around quickly to ascertain that he wasn't being watched, he dumped his stew into a flower bed.

As he turned, he thought he saw something out of the corner of his eye. He spun around and looked.

Nothing but leaves on a trellis rustling in the breeze.

Funny. He could have sworn he saw someone moving, peering out at him. Nerves and paranoia. That threatening note had obviously bothered him more than he realized.

When he returned and showed off his empty bowl to Haldane with a wink, he sat back down and politely refused an offer from a Creon neighbor to go back up and get a second helping for him.

"I'm waiting for the next course," he explained.

The next course proved much more palatable: a plate of grilled vegetables with some sort of spicy sauce. Brogan found this much easier to eat by not asking the full nature, merely shoveling it down and sipping the *darkan* judiciously.

As soon as his or Haldane's glass showed any sign of lowering, a pitcher was hurried to them and their glasses topped off. It was clear that most of the aliens were already close to inebriation. Most of these guys were absolutely sober as judges on and off duty. This was clearly their time to let their hair down—without any women around to complain about it.

Another two courses—roast meat and then something sweet with specks of fruit dripped on it (again Brogan didn't inquire what the nature of anything was)—and then suddenly Podly was hovering over them wearing a goofy smile. Brogan was coming to loathe that smile. It portended upsetting things. Where oh where was the gruff and grumpy Podly of old?

"And did you have yourselves a good meal then?" Podly inquired. In his cups, he was beginning to sound more and more Irish, if that was possible. Brogan had always enjoyed that about Podly. It made him feel at home. However, at this moment the captain was starting to look and sound like a gigantic leprechaun, a twinkle of mischief in his eye, and that made Patrick Brogan feel very uncomfortable.

"Oh yeah, thanks, sir," said Haldane. "Stuffed! Absolutely bursting."

"Yes, it was—quite an experience," said Brogan diplomatically.

"Good. You boys are workin' in real well. Everyone's warming up to you. That's why the next part of the evening's going to be a bit impromptu." Podly leaned over and put his hands on their shoulders in a proud and possessive manner. "You two are going to make speeches!"

"Speeches!" said Haldane.

"Don't thank me! I know this is a rare and wonderful privilege for Earth people to address an audience, and I know that you Terrans love to talk. So before anything else happens I'm going to put you up there and you can just talk away."

Brogan blinked. "About *what,* sir?"

"Why, the honor and thrill of being here. The joy of participating in these revels—whatever comes up. Just be prepared for me to call you."

And then the Creon was gone on his merry way, heading toward a podium and mike that were even now being assembled at the end of the room.

Haldane turned to Brogan, looking a little pale. "What I'm afraid of is that what comes up will be my dinner."

Brogan's stomach grumbled uneasily.

CHAPTER

"Thank you. Thank you very much," said Patrick Brogan with a bow, acknowledging the applause of his sudden audience. The catcalls and the table-banging, he supposed, were part of the accepting noises, but he had a few problems with the tossed fruit. "It's an honor being here." He dodged a particularly ripe peach-type thing which spattered against the wall behind him, slopping down gooily. "Uhm—I'm afraid I don't have anything prepared, or I'd have a joke to tell about Captain Podly. But then I suppose you've heard them all."

A great bellow of approving laughter filled the assemblage.

It was an oddly comforting sound.

Haldane, sitting alongside him, looking chary of any thrown organic matter, gave him the A-OK sign.

"Just on the way up here, I was thinking to myself—between paroxysms of stage fright"—(laughter) "what a brave step you've taken here. You're allowing a strange creature from another planet to share in some of your most important and personal rituals."

A sound like something from some gigantic whoopee cushion interrupted. Great gushes of laughter and chuckles, and clamoring of cups and tableware resulted. Brogan, unfazed, waited for this to die down and then continued. He was getting used to the raucous spirits being expressed by these Creon and Tarn males. He'd had an inkling of it in the loud and active nightlife he'd had to police on Demeter City. Seeing it now, among his police force colleagues, normally professional, brave, and workaday, actually made him like them more: it gave him a sense of their depths.

Maybe now he had the opportunity to connect with them, show them an inkling of human depths.

"Demeter City is a brave experiment. The Universe is a very big place—but with progress, and more new life and varieties of intelligence being discovered, we're all starting to learn what we of Earth have known for a very long time: When there are differences, there is much potential for conflict.

"Officer Jack Haldane and I are here, now, to learn about you, to be a part of your number—and to bring back the experience and knowledge that will help all of humankind adjust to the ambitious goal of living in harmony with the many fascinating and worthwhile races of the galaxy. There are many differences, yes, but also much in common. We have come here to help you celebrate and honor both."

Brogan went on to speak a little more of his deepest feelings in the matter and his goals. Even as he spoke, he realized that it was a spiritual thing with him, and the sound of his own voice, filled with such hope and courage and pure goals, was infinitely reassuring to his soul.

"In conclusion, let me especially thank Captain Podly," he said finally. "His is a brave, progressive heart. His kind of attitude is the harbinger of the brave new Universe ahead of us."

He turned to Podly at the table below him. The captain was lying head down on his table. The silence that met the end of Brogan's speech was interrupted by an abrupt, sawlike sound: Podly's snores.

Taken aback, Brogan looked out at the rest of his audience.

Everyone was asleep.

Stunned, Brogan went down and sat by Haldane, who, thankfully, was still awake although looking a little dazed by the *darkan* he'd imbibed.

"They've passed out," said Brogan.

"Ah, don't take it personally. You know, maybe they're just not ready for serious and constructive speeches. Maybe, when you spend your life dealing with dead serious stuff like crime and death and drugs and threats to people and safety, you just want to forget stuff like brotherhood and instead

just practice it in jolly oblivion." He winked at
Brogan. "I've got an idea."

Just as Brogan realized that Haldane had collected things under his seat, Haldane reached for
and started throwing them: ripe fruit and vegetables.

Messily, they splattered the frontmost ranks of
the sleepers.

"Hey, guys. Wake up!" yelled Haldane. "Party's
not over yet, is it?"

Consciousness restored to the dreamers, a cry
went among them. Sound hands reached for
organic matter. Laughter swelled and a hail of
stuff darkened the air.

"And for my speech, I have just two words,"
cried Haldane. "Food fight!"

Brogan ducked a hurled piece of fruit.

The fight ended when enough of the group were
laughing so hard, they lay upon their backs. The
sight of all these Creons and Tarns in their female
attire, rolling about in a messy mass of food, rip-
pling with laughter, was a sobering experience for
Patrick Brogan.

He decided to remedy that slightly by actually
drinking his brew.

Yes, he thought as the cool, rich, liquid coated
his nerves and his slightly hurt feelings, *absolutely
ridiculous, all of this, but maybe Haldane has
finally hit upon the secret: Don't think about joining in, just do it.*

In fact, as Podly struggled up from his laughter,
coated with juice and joy, and Brogan finished off

his large cup of brew, he made an interesting observation. This outfit he wore was actually comfortable. He *liked* wearing a dress.

Well, after a drink or two, anyway.

Podly held up his big hand. "An excellent jape! Thank you, my brothers. Thanks to our new members Jack Haldane and Patrick Brogan, we are truly getting into the spirit of these rites. Now then—who knows what happens next!"

"The song!" cried a suddenly alert participant, his voice piping with pleasure.

"Yes. The song of songs!"

"The tune of tunes!"

"The sound of sounds!"

Voices rose, Tarn and Creon alike, to join in an excited clamoring.

Whatever it was that was next was certainly popular. Brogan looked around at the dozens of aliens—no, strike that, he thought. Dozens of *people,* newly aroused from their lethargy, eyes glowing with eagerness.

Haldane shrugged. "Heck. I like music as much as the next guy. I'm in for it."

The drink had put Brogan in a distinctly better mood. He found himself not merely without trepidation, but oddly expectant. Still, a nagging voice of caution kept him refusing the drinks offered him. There was that threat he had to consider, and although the hall was full of cops sworn to preserve the peace, none of them were exactly in a preserving posture at the moment. Besides, there certainly wasn't much peace going on here, anyway.

"Splendid!" said Podly. "Bring on the vat!"

The same group of wide-shouldered Creons who had escorted the stew container hustled off. Within a very short time, they returned, rolling out a similarly shaped vessel, only this one contained a roiling, queasy-colored viscous fluid.

"Who shall be first?" asked Podly.

There were many volunteers.

Lots were drawn, and a hardy soul—a particularly chunky Creon, was marched forward.

"And what is to be *your* song?" asked Podly.

"'Dream of My Heart'!" said the Creon.

Roars of approval met his choice.

"Sir," said Podly. "Your ladle."

He handed the large, spoonlike thing over. The Creon dipped into the mucousy stuff, pulled out a large portion. It drooled over the edges and down the Creon's mouth and front as he sopped the gunky stuff up.

He licked his lips.

The assembly waited expectantly.

"What's going to happen?" Haldane asked Podly.

"Just wait a moment for the stuff to react with all the brew the man has had," replied Podly.

Brogan watched. Within seconds, he began to notice a difference. The man's abdomen was *expanding*. When it had reached a certain size, the Creon grinned and then opened his mouth.

A small burp emerged.

"Testing," said Podly. "Here comes the show."

The man took a quick breath and then proceeded with the longest eruction that Patrick

Brogan had ever heard in his life. Nor was it any simple long burp, but a well-modulated emission of sound and gases that the creature somehow molded to create the most grotesque music he'd ever heard in his life.

When he was through, a full minute later, the house exploded with applause. The Creon bowed, and then took his seat.

"Who's next?" asked Podly.

"You, Podly!"

"Yes, you!"

"Sure, Podly. We sure would enjoy that."

Podly raised an eyebrow. "Would you now? Well, thank you very much. I *will* go next." The Creon stumped over to the vat, lifted the ladle, and took a hefty portion. When he was finished knocking it back he turned to his audience.

"In honor of our new members, I should like to do a song that very much appeals to me from the planet Earth." He smiled over at Brogan and winked. "And now: 'Danny Boy.'"

Podly's tuneful eruction commenced.

CHAPTER

It was one of the most
bizarre noises that Jane Castle had ever heard in
her life.

The truly odd thing, though, was that she recognized the tune it seemed to try to carry.

"Is that 'Danny Boy'?" she said in disbelief.

"What?" whispered Took.

Ted Bickford leaned an ear closer to the window,
looking thoughtful. "Why yes—I believe it is
'Danny Boy'—although I'm afraid that even as we
speak, all dead Irish tenors are turning in their
graves—and living ones are headed there."

It was enough to see so many of her colleagues
drunk and wearing female apparel. But hearing
Captain Podly, her stern and grumpy boss, emitting the most outrageous and lengthy burp that
she had ever before been witness to—

All in a wobbly key of G.

She had her recording equipment on. She got the whole sad song. She made sure she got some close-ups of some of the principals involved in this strange male-bonding ritual—including Brogan and Haldane.

Patrick and Jack looked particularly fetching in their gowns. Good design, good work. She was almost envious. She knew that she would look damned good in one of those, with her hair down, showing some shoulder. The damnable thing was that those guys looked pretty damned good, too.

Ah well! Perhaps it was good for their consciousness raising.

She happened to hear a slight click. Her senses were particularly attuned this evening because of the covert nature of this activity. She might not have heard the sound under normal circumstances: it was very faint.

She turned around. Ted Bickford was standing immediately behind her. He had his gun out. On the top of the gun he had placed a scope. Now, he was sighting through the scope, in the general direction of Podly.

"Hey! What—"

"Just checking it out," whispered Bickford cheerfully. "Night/day adjustable vision. If we're camping out tonight, you don't know who or what we're going to run into. Just preparing." He handed her the gun, then showed her a clip of ammunition. "See. Not even loaded."

Took was frowning. She looked alarmed by the incident, but said nothing.

"Ted, I know you're a military sort," she whispered. "But you just don't go around flashing guns like that."

Bickford looked sheepish. "Okay. Maybe you're right. Sorry." He pursed his lips thoughtfully, shrugged. "Look, maybe you'd better keep it for now, huh? I guess maybe I like to play with it too much."

"Yes. That's probably a good idea." She put the gun into her carrying case. "If we get charged by a raving and drooling Jek-beast, I'll give it back to you."

"Especially if it's in a dress," quipped Bickford. He seemed very relaxed and affable, clearly enjoying the bizarre sight inside the assembly hall.

She relaxed and went back to work, alarm gone as she got all this down for posterity.

Oh yes, she thought. *Why don't you do a little bit of Jimmy Cagney's George M. Cohan, Podly? A little dance to go along with the song would be very appropriate.* She could sell this tape to the Galactic Entertainment Services.

What would she call it?

'I'M A CREON DOODLE DANDY'?

No.

'MONDO SPACE PRECINCT'?

Tee-hee.

Podly finished the belching song and the crowd went wild with applause. Jane had to turn down her mikes. The sound was simply thunderous.

This was actually fine with her, since obviously every single soul inside the building was very much a part of this peculiar *gestalt* and paying no attention to the possibility that a woman might be outside the window, recording all this.

After the applause died, Podly pulled Haldane and Brogan up to the vat.

"All right, gentle beings. Let's see what kind of music Earth men can make," said the captain.

The crowd seemed very much in favor of the suggestion.

Jane could not help but giggle as she saw Jack turn totally white at the prospect.

Brogan, however, nixed the idea immediately.

"No way, Captain."

"Why not?"

"Look, I'm no doctor, but I understand enough about human anatomy to know that those kinds of gases building up in our abdomens could rupture something. You Creons and Tarns must have incredibly hardy gastrointestinal systems."

Podly looked quite pleased at the compli-ment. "Yes, particularly Creons. Although Tarns, I must say, have come a long way over the years."

A fruity belch was his reply.

"Very well," said Podly. "We don't want to kill you. However, we *do* intend to regale you with the absolutely most wonderful music you have ever heard in your life."

"Mind if we sit down for this one?" said Brogan.

"Mind if we have another drink for this one?" said Haldane.

Brogan allowed his beer mug to be filled, but only sipped it. He looked quite sober. Jack, on the other hand, looked to Jane as though he'd had more than his share of drink this night. Jack wasn't usually a drinking kind of guy. Now Jane could see why. She would have thought the whole thing much funnier if she hadn't had an alcoholic uncle. Jane had some wine and champagne at times, but that was about it. She was too aware of the damage that too much drinking could do to a person.

She watched and recorded as a large majority of the Creons and Tarns lined up. One by one they passed by the vat. Two of the heavily muscled Tarns ladled out the viscous fluid into cups. All the participants waited until everyone had been served, and then formed stacked groups, facing Podly.

Upon a signal, they all downed their drinks. Jane could hear the glug-glug of their drinking: it would definitely be on tape in all its echoing glory, this distinguished male bizarreness.

The reaction was almost immediate. Slowly their abdomens swelled. Podly watched all this with great attention to detail, obviously awaiting the optimum moment.

When stomachs protruded so much that the hall looked like a maternity ward, Podly signaled.

Forty some mouths opened.

Forty tuned, attenuated belches erupted into being, swaying into a braying joyful chorus. Podly swung his hands about, directing this impromptu chorale.

The results were truly startling. It was like no music that Jane Castle had heard before. Oddly enough, it was rather stirring.

When she was a child, Jane Castle had visited the American South. In Alabama, she had stayed at a large farm. At the back of the farm was a pond. Sweet summer nights she had lain awake, listening to the bullfrogs serenade the stars and moon amid the dear honeysuckle breezes.

The alien chorus sounded something like those bullfrogs, only with more structure. The voices rang with bass and baritone life, with humor and vigor, with gutsy self-awareness and celebration.

Jane was simultaneously thrilled and startled at the noise. It was disturbing and yet attractive. The notion of an art form involving burping was absolutely offensive to her sensibilities—but she felt something of these people's souls here, and it was a stunning feeling. For a brief moment, she was almost ashamed for eavesdropping on this bizarre private ceremony.

But then she remembered her mission, the important cause that had brought her here, and duty steeled her once more.

She turned to Took. "I see now why they have to come out here in the middle of nowhere."

Took looked upset, baffled, and confused—and as though she would far rather be anywhere else than witnessing this event.

Ted was extremely intrigued by the whole thing. Jane just hoped he wasn't going to puff himself up and join in.

She looked back inside as the symphony of voices growled down into a final gassy gurgle. Brogan and Haldane clapped, both almost looking like they, too, had wanted to join in.

She checked her equipment, turned it off. "That's enough for now. No telling when this is going to break up. If we get caught, this will have been for nothing."

Took nodded.

With their help, she packed the equipment and slunk off back toward the gate.

The night had gone cold, and so they sat around a portable heater that gave off a lot of heat but very little light.

By then, they'd covered their hopper with branches. They were in a dip in the land on the verge of a forest by the field where they had landed. It was a good hiding place.

"Well, I could complain about the food," said Ted, spooning the last bit of the vegetable hash out of his plastic container. "But we are camping. However, I must say, I can't complain about the company."

"Thanks," said Jane, leaning against the bole of a tree. Although the temperature had gone down, they had thermal clothing—and besides, it was rather bracing. They could sleep outside tonight in their bags, each taking turn as sentry.

Jane felt very good indeed. So far, their mission was a success. She just hoped it continued in this most excellent vein. "We appreciate your being here, Ted."

Took said nothing. She merely toyed with her mostly full container.

"Thanks. I'm having a very educational time. Also it's very fulfilling spending meaningful time with you, Jane." He got a wry look on his face. "I have absolutely no compunction about exposing the kind of antics that go in this exclusive society. This whole business just makes me more sure that fully integrated society is the way to go—not just on Earth, but in the Universe."

"Absolutely. Thanks for the solidarity here, Ted. Intelligence conquers sexism." Jane raised a fist and laughed good-naturedly.

"I'm only hoping I can get a cut of the money you make on vids with this stuff."

Took looked up, alarmed. "You mentioned nothing about selling your recordings."

Ted chuckled. "Oh, I don't think she will, will you, Jane? But it would make quite a splash, wouldn't it?"

Jane started giggling. It was all she could do not to fall over laughing. Out of respect for Took, though, she restrained herself. Took seemed to be bothered by something that she'd seen tonight. For some reason she didn't get the full hilarity and absurdity of what they'd observed.

"Yes. Brogan and Haldane would be in such demand for *Vogue* covers!"

Ted laughed at that, but again Took remained stone-faced.

"Did you feel any male affinity with what you

saw tonight?" asked Jane. "Any resonance tingling the basic root of your masculinity?"

Ted's handsome face moved into a thoughtful expression. "I have to tell you, I guess any guy enjoys the idea of getting together with his buddies, drinking too much, and making a fool of himself. To that extent, mea culpa. But it was interesting to see that alien rites could have such affinities for your friends. Obviously they enjoyed wearing those dresses and bonding with their Creon and Tarn counterparts immensely."

"Have you ever done anything like that?" asked Jane.

"Hey. I'm just here to help you establish equality— and to spend some time with you, Jane." He held up his hands. "Also, maybe to make up for not being in contact with you for so long. The deal is that you don't turn those cameras and tape recorders on me, okay?"

"Deal," said Jane.

"Good. Now if you will excuse me, I need to commune with some of my more basic nature—a little deeper in those woods. Mind if I take my gun with me, Jane, just in case I meet the Altorian equivalent of a lion, tiger, or bear?"

"Sure, Ted." She pulled the gun out of the bag and handed it over to him. "Just don't shoot off anything, okay?"

"It's all far too precious for that, Jane." He took the gun and carefully crept up the bank toward the woods.

When he was gone, Took turned to Jane. "You let him have that gun back?"

"Sure. Why not?"

Took's eyes were wide. Her third eye was clamped shut hard. "I don't have good feelings about that guy, Jane. I really wish you hadn't brought him along?"

"Ted? Oh, he's fine. Truly. And I thought we might need a cohort. A strong male back to carry the equipment. What can I say? Exploitation."

"I'm serious. What do you really know about him?"

"Took, I told you. Very intimate things. He's an old flame. I think he'd like to start up again. I'm not so sure about that—but I know he's harmless. Why are you so upset? Some kind of psychic alarm going off?"

"No."

"You mean, you're not getting negative readings from Ted."

"No negative ones, and that puzzles me, because my intuition doesn't like him much. That gun business . . . What was that all about?"

"Oh, a male plaything maybe. You know guys and guns. Penis symbol and all that. Maybe it made him feel safer when he saw all those guys bonding in there. Maybe he was threatened. I don't know." She leaned closer. "What I do know is that we, as females, cannot afford to discourage males who take us and our causes seriously."

"Did it occur to you that this Ted Bickford may just be an opportunist?"

"Oh, absolutely. I let him sleep in my bag, you can bet he's going to take his opportunity very seriously."

"No. That's not what I mean. I'm just wondering if he's got a different agenda, that's all."

"Like what? I told you, I met him years ago. We had a relationship. He's back. You mean, he set up that relationship two years ago just so he could come out here to Dreek Island now and watch Podly and company put on dresses?"

"I don't know. Maybe you're right. It's just a feeling, that's all. And it's odd, because I usually operate on psychic input, not feelings."

"So you're saying you could be wrong."

"I suppose so."

"I'm going to be watching him, though."

"Oh. Do so. Absolutely."

There was a moment of tense silence between them.

Jane knew very well that Took didn't really want to be here. She'd almost had to drag the Tarn along. But, she reasoned, it was good for her. She was just so damned easygoing and sweet and accepting of things. She had to see the truth about how life worked sometimes.

After a while, Took said, "It's taking Bickford an awfully long time out there."

"Maybe he got lost."

As though this were his cue, they heard a snapping and the sound of branches being pushed aside.

Soon Ted was sitting back beside them at the fire.

"Got a little lost. Sorry." He smiled. "Were you worried?"

Took looked at Jane pointedly. "Yes."

"Captain. Are you okay?"

The captain had just collapsed heavily into a chair.

The songs had long since died and now the assemblage had dissolved into separate groups, talking among themselves. Brogan and Haldane had been sitting at a table, just waiting for the word that they could be dismissed so that they could go back to their room and get some sleep.

Then "Thump!" Podly collapsed into his chair.

The big head leaned back, eyelids at half-mast. "Oh dear. Yes, I think so."

"Overindulgence," said Haldane.

"Oh, yes, definitely," said the big Creon. "But—very odd."

"What, sir."

The bleary eyes blinked. "It was as though a black *shnarg* just scratched my burial tree."

CHAPTER

When Liz Brogan got up in the morning, she felt as though a black cat had just walked over her grave.

Creepy. Shivers. Stuff like that.

She'd had a nightmare last night. It was all vague and musty, this memory, but it had something to do with getting chased by zombies in rotting powerball uniforms, trailing some kind of sugary green slime. Somewhere in that dream (though she couldn't remember exactly where), that thing she'd found in the park, that rock-jewel, erupted out of the ground, grew exponentially, and began throbbing with some kind of eerie mystical power.

"Help me," it had said in a squeaky voice.

She rubbed the sleep dirt out of her eyes, pulled off her sheets, and went to the dresser drawer where she'd put the thing. She picked it up and examined it.

Nope. No vibrations. Nothing. How odd, though. Somewhere, in the back of her mind, there was still a throbbing something that said that this thing was important, and that she'd better do something about it—at least to find out if her hunch (and her dream) was correct.

After using the bathroom and dressing, she went to Matt's room. Matt was still sleeping, of course. It wasn't a school day and Matt had burned the midnight oil at his computer or reading or something.

"Hey, Matt." She shook his shoulder.

"Whu . . . ?" Not moving, just being his usual slug self.

"Matt, wake up. This is real important."

The slug turned over, raised himself up from his pillow, hair draped in bleary eyes. "Unggh . . ." He spoke eloquently. "What do *you* want?"

"This rock here"—she thrust it into his face—"the one I showed you before. Are you getting anything from it, anything at all?"

"What are you talking about, Liz?"

"I think it gave me a nightmare last night. Anyway, it kind of gives me the creeps."

Matt pushed himself up and stared at her as though she was going out of her mind. "You're waking me up for this."

"It's some kind of alien thing and it feels important. Mom's already at work today and Dad's off at his thing. What have you got planned today?"

He thumped back into sleeping mode. "What I was doing before you interrupted me."

"In other words, nothing much. Okay. So then you can help me."

"Liz, I've got better things to do. Now scram." He pulled his pillow under his head and hugged it, tuning out his little sister and the world.

Hmm, thought Liz Brogan. This looked like a real challenge.

One more appeal to whatever he used for intelligence.

"Matt. All I want you to do is to take the transport with me to the precinct and have somebody look at this. It could be important. I'm getting a real sense of immediate danger. A Tarn should look at it."

"Hrmmmff," said Matt.

"All the Tarns say I've got some kind of embryonic psychic power, Matt."

"Yeah. They say that about *all* humans. But right now, this bit inside me needs a rest."

"But they say I'm especially adept."

"Yeah, right. Go away, Liz."

So much for that. Liz looked around at the possibilities. Hmm. There was his baseball bat. No, that might put him in deeper unconsciousness. Her eyes scanned . . .

Ah-ha!

She went over to his computer. She booted it up and the screen came on in an incandescent splash of colored graphics.

"Fee fie foe fum," said an abrupt voice, "I smell a stranger dumb!"

She tapped a few keys. "Whoops," she said. "Matt, you know I think I accidentally hit the DELETE JUST ABOUT ALL STUPID COMPUTER GAMES code."

Matt was up and awake in a snap.

Orrin the Creon sipped at his hot drink and made a face. He reached for a packet of antacid and chewed some. His abdomen gurgled a plaint, subsided somewhat, and he got back to the task at hand.

A report, as usual. It was up there on his screen, waiting to be filled out. Simple robbery down in the Snart District on Demeter City. Perps apprehended. No bloodshed. He had all the notes from the officers involved. Should be a piece of *ga* cake, right? He'd done plenty of the things in his years here at the precinct. Still, it was irksome. If his partner Romek wasn't on vacation, maybe he would have been able to palm it off on him.

He scratched the tangle of orange fuzz above his ears and grunted. Boring boring boring, yes. But that wasn't the principal problem. The main difficulty was that he was feeling kinda lousy about this whole Dreek Island thing.

Mainly because he hadn't been able to go this year. He'd had to take a few weeks sick leave earlier this year, so he had to be a desk jockey while lots of his buds were out carousing and playing there. He always had a good time on Dreek, and he went every time he could. It wasn't as if they were kicking him out of the organization. He just hadn't realized how *left out* he'd feel when he couldn't go this year.

Everyone was getting attention but him. Even Jane Castle—the poor homely thing—had a male clearly interested in her. He'd stopped in to collect her just recently. What was his name? Dickbird? Something like that.

He sighed and reached for his drink.

"Officer Orrin?"

Orrin jumped. Damn! Too much stimulant. His nerves were jangled.

He swung around toward the piping voice that had called his name and found himself staring at Liz Brogan, Lieutenant Brogan's daughter. Behind her, hands hooked in pockets, was Matt, looking disgusted and bored.

"Liz," said the Creon. "What are you doing here?"

"I need some help, Officer Orrin. My dad isn't here, and you've been so kind in the past. I thought we would come to you. We caught a shuttle from the Space Suburb here to the Station House."

She blinked her eyes prettily. Her brother Matt just rolled his eyes, looking thoroughly disgusted at being dragged down here. Guy looked like he'd just crawled out of bed!

Orrin chewed on a lip for a moment.

True, he'd been nice to these kids, but they were wrong. It was only because he respected, no, *liked* their father. In actuality, he didn't care much for kids—of any race. He was a bachelor, he intended to stay that way . . . and he certainly didn't want a lot of contact with the bratty excuses for living beings that children tended to be.

"What's up, Liz?" he said, hesitantly.

"This, Officer Orrin." She thrust forward a small rock of some kind. Orrin took it and examined it. Definitely a rock, but it possessed jewellike surfaces that glimmered with a translucent, amberlike quality. Smoky interior, redolent of prismatic resonance.

"Very pretty," said Orrin. "What does it mean?"

"She found it in the park the other day, and it's giving her nightmares," said Matt in a sardonic, bored manner. "She thinks maybe a Tarn might be able to get some kind of psychic answer to the thing's nature . . . Me, I just told her to call the Psychic Hotline."

"I just know it's something," said Liz. "And I've got this feeling that it's an item of great importance."

Orrin leaned back, causing his chair to squeak. He ogled the rock-jewel, hefted it thoughtfully. "Well, folks. I don't feel anything. But then, I ain't exactly psychic either." He swiveled his chair around and tapped on his keyboard. "Tell you what. Let me see who's on duty." He punched in a code. Names were coughed up on the screen.

"Somebody *real* sensitive to psychic vibrations," urged Liz, leaning over the desk annoyingly. She almost knocked Orrin's drink over. "Sorry."

"Well, a lot of our Tarn psychic heavy hitters are

out in—ah, well, *training* with your father and Jack Haldane. But looks like we could always go to Janar."

"Janar?"

"Yeah. He's a little older than most of us, works in records. Knows a lot about Tarn stuff . . ." He scratched at his fuzz again. "Yeah, and you know, whenever we lose somethin' around here, we go down and see old Janar, he walks around a bit, talks to the last person who's seen it, and we usually find it."

Liz Brogan's eyes glowed. "Yes. He'll do just fine."

"Okay. I'm just about off shift anyway." Orrin got up, and gestured with one of his big hands. "Come on, kids. This way."

Yeah. This won't take long.

Anyway, it was the least he could do for his friend from Earth, Patrick Brogan.

Liz watched as the older Tarn turned the jewel-stone over in his wrinkled fingers. He looked to her like he should be retired and off enjoying his sunset years somewhere: long grey hair flowed down to settle thinly upon his police collar. His face was lined and mottled, but his eyes were clear and sharp. He smelled of jasmine and old leather.

He sniffed the thing, rolled it against his face, shook it, and then placed it against an ear.

His third eye opened slowly, then closed suddenly.

"My goodness, Liz Brogan," said the Tarn, turning to the twelve-year-old. "Wherever did you get this?"

Liz told him. "What is it?"

"Very odd. A soul-jewel in the middle of a public park. That's the strangest thing . . ."

"Hey, you know, I'm actually getting interested," said Matt, peering over his sister's shoulder. "So don't keep us in suspense, Mister Janar."

"Humans don't see these . . . nor Creons either. They're deeply personal to Tarns." He looked up from the soul-jewel to his audience. "Each Tarn keeps one of these in a recessed part of his body. It's kind of like a memory node, only it contains much more than that. Imprinted upon each are psychic identities, personal data, and life-reflections. Sounds, images . . . brain recordings of the life that was lived. When a Tarn dies, this is ejected. But generally only hours later in the presence of other Tarns, during a ceremony. It is placed into the Collective, becoming rather like what you might call a part of a racial memory. So you can see why I'm surprised you found it in a park!"

"So either it was taken there," said Liz, "or some Tarn died there, and the soul-jewel was lost."

"Either way, it's highly unusual for this to happen," said the old Tarn. "Either way, it bodes ill. And you're quite correct, young humans . . . There is a bad scent about this soul-jewel. A jewel without its owner has either been stolen from the Collective, or was never there in the first place."

"What do we do?" said Matt. Whatever one said about her brother's general apathy and disdain toward most things, when a mystery popped up, he was interested.

"I wish I could help identify the owner and read this thing. Alas, I cannot, nor do we have the necessary equipment here." The Tarn shook his head. "No, you'll have to go to the planet's surface for that. You'll have to go down to Demeter City. The Collective Annex, to be precise. Here, I'll write the address down." He found a scrap of paper and a pencil and started scribbling.

"We can't go down to the surface unless someone takes us," said Matt.

For a moment, Liz felt vexed and frustrated. Dad was gone, and no way was Mom going to get out of work to ferry them down to Demeter City. She probably wouldn't even want to give permission for the enterprise.

Then inspiration hit her.

"Officer Orrin," she said. "You said you were about to get off work."

"Yes . . . but . . ." Orrin blinked. "Oh, no! I can't possibly take you down to Demeter City. I . . . I . . . I just can't."

"But it's important," said Matt.

"Yeah, and our dad said that if we ever had to turn to anyone, it was his good friend, Orrin the Creon."

"You really should, Orrin," said Janar. "The sense I get is that the information on this soul-jewel may be vital."

Orrin looked at the two sets of double eyes staring at him expectantly, then the one set of triple eyes.

"Okay," he said, sighing. "But I'm taking you down, doing this, and then bringing you *right back!*"

Liz hugged him.

CHAPTER

"Up and at 'em, boys!"

The gruff voice tore through the morning dimness like burlap ripping.

Jack Haldane woke up and the second voice to greet him was that of a hangover: "Hey, jerk. You drank too much last night. Heh-heh. I'm going to be hanging around for a while so I'm just going to wash my hands on your tongue here and punch the grey matter a bit. Oh, and mind if I use your stomach for an ashtray? I love to smoke rotten cee-gars. Hey hey."

In the bed beside him, Patrick Brogan groaned. "Captain Podly, you kept us up half the night. Have a heart."

Haldane opened his mouth to eloquently support this argument, but only "Unghhhh," emerged.

"I'm not going to take any excuses," bellowed the

Creon, back to his usual form. "This is all a part of what you've accepted. You want to get in some *shrat* before the sun gets too hot, don't you."

"Sir, the weather report was calling for clouds and maybe a storm," said Brogan.

"All the more reason to get in that *shrat*. Gods, I love that game. Can't wait to get at it. And I'm not going to let a couple of sluggards of your ilk keep me from it! Now get up and get dressed. See you down for first meal in fifteen minutes or I personally will come up and haul you down."

The door banged shut.

"Well, at least the old Podly is back," said Brogan. "The affable Podly's a little too much to bear sometimes."

Haldane buried his head in a pillow. *"Life* is too much to bear sometimes."

"Hmm. Do I sense a slight morning-after attitude?"

"Brogan. I feel like someone stole my brain and viscera, took them out on the town, dumped them into a cement mixer—and then shoveled the result back inside the cavities."

"Hmm. Well, I've got some Aspirin Plus that my wife packed for me."

"What's the Plus?"

"Just about everything legal under numerous suns."

"I want the whole bottle."

Brogan gave him three. Those, along with a couple of glasses of water and a hot shower, made Haldane feel at least *sub*human.

Even so, they didn't make it down in fifteen minutes and so they found themselves before a glowering Podly.

"You're keeping me from my game," he said, looking down at his wrist chronometer and tapping a foot.

"Sorry, Captain," said Jack. "I drank too much last night. Don't feel too good. But you know, I'm so charged with the idea of playing this *shat*—"

"*Shrat.*"

"Yeah, right. That game. So I'm looking forward to it so much that I *made* myself get out of bed."

The Creon's face softened. "You're really looking forward to it?"

"Absolutely," said Haldane with as much sincerity as he could muster from his tired self. "And I know that Brogan is, too. Right, Patrick?"

"Yes. I guess I am."

Podly nodded. "I can understand how you feel about the drink." He gestured over to the Creons and Tarns, busily eating their breakfast. "More than one of us are a little under the weather for that very same reason, Haldane. That's why there's a little extra something in the gruel this morning." A wry smile curled the edge of his mouth. "Little boost, don't you know."

"Hmmm. Gruel," said Brogan. "My favorite."

Podly shuffled them along to the service line, where they collected their bowls and headed for yet another vat. A Creon in a chef's hat happily doled out a plop of coagulated green and yellow from the vat.

At first Haldane thought the little black specks in the gruel were raisins. Then his fogged brain remembered that there were no raisins on Altor. He looked closer. The "raisins" had many little legs, a segmented body, and fuzz and antennae.

"Bugs!" he said.

"Well," said Brogan looking up from his own breakfast with a sour but resigned expression. "Podly *did* promise us a little something extra."

Hopefully, a something extra that would help his hangover, Haldane thought as he brought up his first spoonful.

That, or it was designed simply to empty his system of whatever was still banging around down there.

Haldane sighed, held his nose against the gruel's slightly off smell, and fed it to himself.

Yum-yum.

Yeah. Right.

In the distance, over the ocean, Patrick Brogan could see the dark of gathering clouds.

He didn't like the look of it. Storms on tropical islands could be pretty fierce. However, Captain Podly seemed bothered not at all by the portents of foul weather.

"It's a simple enough game," he said in his growly, didactic tone. "You hit a ball as far as you can, and you try to get it in a hole."

"Great!" said Jack Haldane. "Sounds like golf. I can golf okay."

Podly speared him with a cold, sharp look. "I

said simple, not stupid. *Shrat* is simple in principle, but it has levels and skills and meaning which your silly golf cannot possibly pretend to. There are subtle as well as vibrant complexities to the numerous challenges present in *shrat*. Please, if you value your position among your peers here in Dreek Island, do not compare it to golf."

Brogan said nothing. *Shrat* sounded a lot like golf to him. But if Podly didn't want to hear comparisons, why bring them up?

He and Haldane were dressed in their own casual wear of pleated khaki slacks, walking shoes, and light cotton shirts. The sky above them was warm and sunny, the only portent of any coming storm the slight ozone taste to the breeze.

Podly, on the other hand, was dressed in some kind of special uniform whose only analog would be the exotic apparel worn by many of the players of that other ball and hole game on the planet Earth, the game whose name could not currently be mentioned.

For starters, he wore a bright crimson-and-purple-checked pantaloons that belled out at the bottoms over high-heeled boots with mirror-shiny buckles. Above his wide chintz belt was a frilled alien-paisley shirt, filled with sparkling buckles and bows. At his neck was a bow tie worthy of the Mad Hatter, flowing and wide and convoluted with bright designs in clashing colors. And at the top of his head he wore a high-topped, visored thing that had perhaps been made by the aforementioned professional. A wobbly, mushroom cap of a thing that looked partially inflated and wholly ridiculous.

Or, at least ridiculous to Brogan's sensibilities. This was an alien planet after all. They didn't exactly follow the standard taste and color codes.

Besides, maybe *shrat outfits had about the same relationship to Altorian fashion that its Earth analog sport's costumery had to general Earth fashion.*

Oh well, he was thinking too much. His duty now was just to learn this game, get through it, please Podly, and absorb some more alien culture.

"Sorry, sir. Anyway, so what do we do with these clubs if not hit the ball?" The suffering Haldane lifted his "weapon." It was, indeed, just what he had called it: a club. It was a large piece of wood that looked like something a Neanderthal of ancient Earth might wield. There was a thick end, tapering up to a slender end. At the base, though, were odd junctures and protuberances, and Brogan noticed that there were differently angled and shaped carvings upon the bottom as well.

Podly rolled his eyes, which was something indeed to experience. It took a moment or two. "Of course you hit the ball, Haldane. Isn't that what one does in any sport, here, there, and everywhere? Hit some sort of ball."

Brogan, a true-blue Mets fan, thought about that for a moment. Yes, Podly was right. Apparently the Cosmic Force of Creativity, so varied in so many different ways, was pretty much stuck on a single note in terms of these kinds of universal sports.

Then again, in his experience with golf, he sometimes wondered if the Cosmic Force had nothing to do with it, and if indeed it was true that a devious and sadistic Satan existed.

"Yeah. So where do I hit it?"

"I'll show you."

Podly went to his cart and pulled out his own club. He pulled out a huge set of binoculars (which had to be very wide indeed to fit over his big, widely set eyes) and looked out over the rolling field beyond.

"There," he said finally. "Just past that tree's the flag marking the hole. I will go first. In order to hit the ball properly, you must observe and recreate the movements that I perform."

From his bag he took out a ball. It was larger than a golf ball, and it was not precisely spherical. In fact, it looked a bit wobbly. However, Brogan was certain there had to be reasons for this, so he simply withheld judgment and observed.

From his pocket Podly produced a rock with two flat edges. He propped the floppy ball upon this and whisked the club back and forth a meter away from it.

"Now, notice that I am using the very flat edge of my *hrab*," said Podly. "This is to get the maximum distance."

Haldane opened his mouth, doubtless to point out how similar this was to golf's "driver" concept. But Brogan intercepted this gaffe with a pointed look. Haldane got it and kept his mouth shut.

"Fascinating," said Haldane.

"It's a true science, what you are about to see. It's also an art and an important ritual."

"I don't suppose you could ward off those clouds on the horizon with some of that ritual," said Brogan.

Podly didn't seem to notice. He seemed too busy getting himself revved up for his game's form of teeing off.

"Hey. How come *you* get the smart remarks?" Haldane asked, stepping up to Brogan's side.

"Because I mutter them out of earshot."

Podly did a kind of deep knee bend and then twisted his head from side to side. Then he set his club to one side, placed his massive head on the ground, and pushed himself into a headstand. While maintaining this position, he blinked his eyes, then opened and closed them rapidly.

"Just for the purpose of enlightenment," said Brogan, "would you mind explaining the point of that particular—ah—ritual?"

"Not at all," said Podly. "Clears the head. Sharpens the mind. Cleans out the wits. Going to need them for this game, gentle beings." He thumped back into place, grabbed hold of the club, swung it back over his shoulder, and then bellowed a warning to any other greens' strollers. "Watch out!"

The club whacked down onto the ball and the ball sailed a far way down the fairway indeed.

"What are they doing now?" asked Took.

Jane Castle adjusted the lens of the telescopic

finder of the vu-recorder to focus on the events occurring. So far they'd all hit their balls in various ways into the bizarre grounds, lost them, found them, holed them, unholed them, and generally seemed to be playing a very confused and even more irrational form of golf.

"Well, right now it looks as though Jack Haldane has lost his ball in sort of quicksand. Right now, Brogan and Podly are trying to fish Jack out before he sinks all the way down."

"Oh dear."

"You want the binoculars?"

"No, that's all right. I don't think I particularly want to see what's going on down there."

"Just more male ritual. Quite something really. Looks as though this game makes golf look reasonable."

They'd gotten up bright and early, waited in foliage, and then followed the gamesters out to their first set of exclusive undertakings. So far, they'd been able to find plenty of rocks and trees and foliage to cover their observations.

"What do you think about this, Ted?"

No answer.

She looked up. Their male counterpart, who had so far been happily lugging their equipment around, was gone. Jane checked her bag.

Ted's gun was gone as well.

CHAPTER

The hopper settled down by the huge, stately building. The bubble top opened and Liz Brogan hopped out, followed shortly by her older brother, Matt.

"Wow!" said Liz.

"Awesome plus," said Matt.

After making sure the hopper was secure, Orrin the Creon got out as well, staring up at the complex before them and its curious architecture. "Yep—say what you like about the Tarns, when it comes to important buildings they can do up a real grand job."

Liz had been to Europe a few years ago and seen some of the grand cathedrals there. The Tarn Collective Building reminded her of one of those cathedrals, only on a more circular than rectangular grand design scheme. Towers and spheres hovered about: all in all it looked like a cluster of opaque soap bubbles connected by flying buttresses.

"What part of the building is this guy in?" asked Matt, looking bemused at the wealth of segments, doors, and passageways that comprised the complex.

"I'm not sure," said Orrin. "Liz, you wrote down all the details."

Indeed, Liz was already consulting her pad. Although she had a palmtop computer for tasks such as these, she'd already found that she preferred simply carrying around a small tablet of paper. On this she would jot down not just directions and details such as these, but also thoughts and ideas and descriptions and word sketches of things. Liz had recently decided that becoming a writer was her destiny, and was taking pains to jot down as much as possible. As with everything in her life, writing worked best when it was a contact sport. She got much more satisfaction actually being directly in touch with her words through the medium of pen and paper. She was now a bit of a techno-rebel in this respect. Matt called her a "Luddite." For instance, although she loved to read, she refused to carry the portable "Compu-Books" so popular now on Earth, far preferring paperbacks and such. It was an expensive luxury and her dad complained about the cost of importing, but Sally Brogan was keenly supportive of her daughter's literary ventures and she humored her. Besides, Mom had secretly confided that she'd never really approved of computerized books anyway. "It just doesn't seem like a real book, somehow, if you can't bend the pages, hold it, mangle it. Printed words on paper seem so much more permanent."

Paper was a subject that had entered Liz's mind when Janar had suggested they come down and visit the Collective. She'd read before that Tarns didn't use paper much, and had none at all within the entire building complex. Instead they used special psychically charged items to store records as such, allowing the moods and music of the recordings to mingle with the rest of the contents of the complex. That was fine and fascinating. However, to Liz, who still had strong memories of daylong jaunts in old-fashioned Earth libraries, browsing, reading, immersing herself in the joys of written words on paper, it seemed as though books had their own kind of psychic charge, readable only to those lucky human beings who loved them.

An experience, then.

A mission and fodder for her newly churning journalistic and literary mill.

One of the reasons she was so excited about coming down to the Collective was that she'd have something truly interesting to describe and write about. Even now, she was forming the right word chains to describe what she was seeing, feeling, touching, smelling, tasting.

"You know," said Matt, for once echoing her own thoughts, "I don't test particularly high for psychic aptitude, but this place is speaking to me." He shook his head with awe. "It just somehow *feels* important."

"Oh, important it is, all right," said Orrin. "It's the center for the Tarn Soul on Demeter City. Of course, they have more back on their home planet. Tarns build these things on any planet where there's more than one Tarn. This is one of the grandest, since it's taken a lot of architectural features from alien cultures around the world." Orrin sighed. "You know, I may just be a Creon blue-collar sort of guy who likes his sports and his brew in the local tavern . . ."

"Joe Sixpack?" asked Liz.

"What?"

"Oh, just an Earth phrase," said Matt. "Ignore her. She collects names and phrases and stuff like other girls collect Barbie accoutrements."

"Barbie?"

Both Liz and Matt looked at each other, then broke out in laughter. "Oh, you don't want to know, Orrin . . ."

"Anyway, it's a real honor for an intelligent being other than a Tarn to be allowed in one of these," continued Orrin. "We should be grateful for the experience."

"Intelligent?" said Liz. "Well, that leaves Matt at the door."

"Hey! Who taught you computer languages?" said an indignant Matt.

"Kids, kids, must you be at each other's throats all the time? Creon children are trained to be very respectful of one another," said Orrin.

"Sibling rivalry," announced Liz, trotting out another phrase that she'd learned recently. "Besides, if I don't keep him humble, his head will just swell until it explodes."

"Really?" said Orrin gravely. "How gruesome. I didn't know you humans had that problem."

They'd already reached the promenade and were now walking through a grand arcade of glass which constituted the foyer and reception area, flanked by Tarn guards.

A tall, regal Tarn in flowing ceremonial garb—azure and chartreuse silk, hanging in odd ruffles and pleats—looked up from a desk at them through spectacles with three lenses. In the distance Liz heard marble library echoes and the shuffles of silence.

"Yes?" said the receptionist.

"Yeah," said Orrin. "This human kid here, Liz Brogan—she's got something that one of your specialists is supposed to take a look at."

The receptionist peered quizzically for a moment at Liz, then looked at Matt with distaste. "Oh. Yes. Allow me to consult my schedule book."

A long sheet of bond plastic sheaths was brought out. It had been scribbled in with some Magic-Marker sort of writing implement: aqua and sepia letters.

"Yes. You are expected. Please proceed down the corridor to the left. Wear these pins." The Tarn receptionist handed over three pins, each holding some sort of burnt orange ornament. "These will be your guides. May I just see the soul-jewel in question as a means of ascertaining your proper identity."

Liz was busy staring down at the orange ornament. Was it her imagination, or was it softly singing—some sort of diminutive insect song?

"Hey, doof. The soul-jewel," prompted Matt with his usual tact and decorum.

Still, it woke Liz out of her reverie. "Uhm—oh yeah. Sorry. Here." She rummaged in her pocket, pulled it out, and handed it over to the old and wrinkled, but definitely authoritative, receptionist. She noticed how fine and sleek and perceptive his slender fingers seemed as they plucked the stone from her palm. He looked down at the thing.

His expression changed from mild boredom to concern mingled with horror.

"Oh! Yes." Quickly, he handed it back, as though it were hot. "Most alarming. You've come to the right place. S'nath will be able to deal with this—" The expression on his face seemed to finish the sentence: "And I'm very thankful that I don't have to be near it anymore."

Orrin ushered them forward in the direction indicated. The two guards stepped out of the way, looking down at the soul-jewel in Liz's hand with the same sort of expression of grim misgivings as the receptionist had shown.

"My guess," said Matt, "from all the data presented to us, is that something real bad happened to the Tarn who used to own this."

"Yeah," said Orrin. "That seems to be the message we're getting. I don't feel nothin' from that thing—but I tell you, the vibes I been gettin' from the Tarns who have gotten near it ain't good at all."

"It's important that we're here," said Liz, voice filled with ostentation. "And it's urgent as well—I just *know* it. We shouldn't dawdle."

"Hey, I'm movin', I'm movin'," said Orrin. "You think I don't want to get this stuff over as soon as possible. I got a hot meal and a ball game waitin' for me at the end of the experience. This place gives me the willies!"

They walked down the hall, their steps echoing in the odd acoustics. Liz felt like Dorothy in the chambers of Oz, headed off to finally see that Wizard.

The corridor was cool, dark, and imposing, with sconces illuminating portraits of impressive Tarn personages, presumably passed on. There was the taste of vanilla in the air, the feel of incense. Liz half expected the sound of chanting monks to insinuate through the passageways at any time now. However, only the sound of distant footsteps and inexplicable susurrations accompanied them.

Soon they came to a place where the corridor split in three different directions.

Orrin scratched his patch of red fuzz and looked down at his pin. "Well, I suppose this is the part where you're supposed to tell us which way to go."

Liz thought she heard the barely audible song increase—and suddenly she felt something stir in her mind.

"That way," she said, pointing off to the right.

"Huh?" said Matt.

"I don't see any pointing green arrows or nothin'," said Orrin, looking down at his pin.

"The pins must be reaching into my mind and showing me the way," said Liz, feeling a total surety about the subject.

"Well, it's all we got to go on," said Orrin. He bowed and gestured. "Please lead on, and we'll follow."

"I don't know," said Matt. "Last time I followed Liz, I ended up in a candy store with a plan to burgle the place!"

"That's not true! I had lots of money. I just got too much in the bag, that's all!" objected Liz.

"Friends, friends," said Orrin. "Please stop bickering. I wish to help you out here, but I've also got a life . . . Yeah . . . I got important things to do."

Liz was going to say something smart and sassy but decided it wasn't a good idea. Mister Orrin was helping them out here, and she wanted to stay in his good graces. "Okay. This way, follow me." She rubbed the pin softly as though it were some magical talisman—this one carrying good omens rather than the grim vibrations surrounding the soul-jewel.

She struck out ahead, leading them down a corridor. This hallway narrowed significantly. The sconces grew fewer and there were no paintings. It seemed a more modern, efficient hallway, and it lost some of the character of the other part of the building. However, it still had that feeling . . . that numinous sense of something vibrant and wonderful and even mystical. Liz opened herself to it, and followed the directions that a small, silent voice gave her in her mind.

Soon, another turn. This time, the pathway angled down, past a series of doors. There was a cooler, darker, wetter feel here. A cavernlike feel of subterranean space and dripping water. Liz half expected to turn a corner and find herself facing a huge underground chamber with stalagmites and stalactites.

Instead, the next turn led down a wider corridor that had a door at the end. Above this door was a sign with the odd squiggly letters above it that embodied examples of the Tarn written language.

Matt said, "What does it say—'Abandon Hope All Ye Who Enter Here'?"

Orrin clearly did not get the Dante's *Inferno* allusion. "No. Actually what it says is: ANALYSIS AND TECHNICAL ADJUSTMENT DEPART-MENT."

"Orrin!" said Liz. "I didn't know you knew the Tarn's written language."

"Part of the training. Gotta know Tarn . . . and I'm learning some Earth languages. The way you Earth people have been moving here in droves, you're gonna take over the place."

"This looks like what we're after," said Matt, ever the assertive one. "Come on. The person we're looking for must be in here."

He pushed open the door and held it open.

The next room was perhaps ten meters wide and softly lit near the front. However, it seemed to go back forever, into a twilight of fuzzy multicolored lights filtered through ragged scrims hanging in layers, like mirrors facing mirrors. There was a smell in here not unlike sandalwood incense.

At the forefront of all this was a long counter hewn from some dark wood sheened to a fine finish.

Something tingled Liz's backbone.

Something very, very *important* was back here. And something rather frightening.

"Hello!" she called tentatively. "Is anyone here?"

Then the lights went out.

Captain Podly uttered
a sharp yelp and then fell over onto his face.

"Captain Podly!" said Brogan. "Are you okay?"

Podly said something rude in his native tongue
and then heaved himself up and brushed sand
from his elaborate costume. The only thing that
looked injured about the Creon was his dignity. He
shook his ruffles, buffed his ridges, and spit out a
mouthful of grit. "Damn," he said, looking up at the
cliff edge by the sand pit. "I hate it when that happens!"

What had happened was that on the Principle
Tertiary of the Secondary Primary of the
Participants' challenge (i.e., what might be called
the fifth hole in golfing nomenclature), Captain
Podly had gotten himself into a bit of a rough spot.
In order to strike the ball properly so that it had

any hope of getting anywhere near its present destination, he had to perch himself near the twisted roots of a *naxa* tree dangling at the edge of a huge *krix* plain. (Haldane had called it a sand trap but had immediately been reprimanded by his superior. "This *is not* golf. I have played golf with diplomats in your Earth park. That is a human game. This is a *Creon* game.") In Brogan's opinion, what you had here, like so many other things he'd discovered in the wilds of the galaxy, was a case of "parallel development." There were so many that it seemed somehow beyond coincidence, headed into destiny. It was nice to know that beings from different planets could relate. As a teenager, when he'd read science fiction, he'd always wondered how exactly *alien* aliens would be and it was a relief to know the answer was *"generally not very."* Intelligent consciousness developed in certain patterns, clearly—patterns which their possessors could relate to and identify with. But *golf*? It all seemed a bit too much. Especially now that he had to play it on an island with his boss in highly unusual conditions indeed.

"Just glad you're okay, sir."

Haldane poked his nose over the side. "Wow! Yeah, I'll say. That was some tumble you took there, Captain. The good news, though, is that you hit your ball a really good distance and it pretty much landed where it was supposed to."

A look of total joy spread over the Creon's features. He raised a celebratory fist and shook it in the air. "Yes!"

He took a step forward and his foot sank into

another hidden hole. "Damn. This sink dirt always gets me."

"Here you go, sir. Let me give you a hand."

Brogan went to his commanding officer and grabbed him by the arm. "You all right, sir?"

"Yes, I'm all right, dammit," snapped Podly, staring down at his trapped boot. "I'm just a little bit stuck, that's all. Happens to me every single time I get myself into one of these damn things." He struggled with his leg, but the thing seemed wedged in tightly.

"We can surely just tug it out if we pull on it together, Podly," said Brogan.

They both leaned over to grab hold of the end of the boot.

At that moment, something whistled past Brogan's ear and smacked into the side of the cliff, spraying up a puff of dust.

"Get down!" he cried.

Podly yelped as Brogan pushed him down. Brogan didn't like the idea of hurting the Creon's leg, but better that than getting perforated by some unseen sniper.

No more bullets whizzed over their heads, however.

"Haldane. You down, guy?"

"As down as down can go," said his partner up on top of the cliff.

"We just got shot at."

"No kidding! I don't see anything on the edge of the forest . . . and frankly in this open air I'm not real inclined to go running out there to find out."

"Just stay in cover and look out." He turned to the prone Podly. "I don't suppose getting potshots taken at you is a part of the game, is it?"

Podly's eyes were wide indeed. "We must get to cover."

"Yes, but there's a sniper up there." Dreek Island sniper. Demeter City sniper. The two concepts were suddenly congruent. What was the connection, though?

"That was no sniper," said Podly.

"I heard a bullet whizz past my ear. It smacked into the bank over there." Brogan pointed.

"That was no bullet," said Podly.

"What are you talking about?"

Podly opened his mouth to explain, but suddenly words were not necessary. Podly pointed over to the bank where the "bullet" had smacked, toward the hole that it had made. Even now, something was emerging from the hole, and since it was close enough (and slow enough this time), Brogan could see just what it was.

It looked like a small armored car with bee wings and a stinger and the face of something out of a bad 1950s monster movie.

"Buzz," it said.

"A *zingak*," said Podly. "Local insect. Not their season, though. I don't know what could have roused it."

As though hearing its name and not particularly liking the way it was pronounced (or spoken without a smile), the *zingak* shook the dust from its wings, turned its trapezoidal oculars toward them, and buzzed louder. Even as he watched the huge bug, its horrific face morphed, turning into something very much like a drill bit, which immediately began to spin.

"Haldane!" cried Brogan. "Sniper alert off! It seems to be some kind of huge homicidal insect."

"And me without my Raid can," Haldane called back.

"What should we do?" asked Brogan.

"The thing can bore a hole straight through a bulletproof vest," said Podly. "Run for cover."

"How's your foot?"

"Thing popped out of the hole. I'm fine."

"Good." Brogan looked around. "Running doesn't seem like a good idea out in the open. Give me your club there."

Podly didn't argue about nomenclature. He just handed the thing over.

"Now start heading for what you think is the safest spot, Podly. We'll follow."

"I can't leave you out here with that thing. And there may be others."

"You just get going, Captain. You don't move quite as quickly as we do."

"True. Very true." The captain got up and started moving surprisingly fast for a Creon, heading off toward the trees.

Just as Brogan had figured it would be, the *zingak* was attracted by Podly's movements.

It launched.

When Patrick Brogan was in high school, he had been on the baseball team. He was an okay shortstop, but what he was best at was hitting a fastball coming straight at him.

Fortunately, although the *zingak* could clearly obtain great speeds, it took awhile to do so. So as it zinged toward Podly, its full acceleration was far from achieved.

Brogan held up his club, judged angle, momentum, trajectory, and then, finally, his gut instinct.

He swung.

The club hit the *zingak* dead on, right on a metallic face.

There was a crunch and a splat, and fluids of a yellow-green ichorish nature flew every which way in a rain of insect gore. All in living queasy Technicolor.

"Got 'im," cried Haldane.

"Good job," called Podly.

"Thanks."

"Game over," said Podly, still plodding toward cover. "That thing's family may still be around. No use tempting fate. Besides, there are plenty of other things to do back at the lodge."

"Sounds great to me!" said Haldane.

"We're right behind you, Podly."

Brogan simply let the club and the disgusting mess on its end drop. Someone could deal with it later. Then he hurried along to catch up with his superior officer.

"Where have you been?" demanded Jane Castle.

Ted Bickford looked surprised at the bite in her

voice. "Out scouting. This is a truly fascinating biome. Just exploring some of it."

"And you took the gun," said Took, frowning.

The trio were still at their observation post above the game course. Jane was quite upset. There had been much confusion and excitement below. Brogan, Podly, and Haldane had just packed up and run for cover after dealing with some kind of murderous insect.

"Why yes," said Bickford. "I thought it would be wise. No telling what kind of wild beast one's going to encounter out there, huh."

Jane was feeling a little more than a slight bit odd. She didn't know if it was the environment and the tension she was under now, or if it was Took's paranoia. In any case, all of her confidence in Ted Bickford's sterling reputation was suddenly vanishing.

Exactly what *did* she really know about this guy anyway that he hadn't told her—or that she'd merely bought on flimsy evidence—or that her glands were telling her. Now, though, that she wasn't under that sway so much, she was honestly wondering one thing: Was this guy who he said he was?

"I can understand your concern for self-defense, Ted. But really you should have told us where you were going," she said.

His good looks creased with concern. "Ah—okay. Sorry to cause you grief, Jane. Just trying to be helpful, just doing what you asked me to do." He handed over the gun. "Here. Take this, if it will make you feel better."

Jane took the weapon. It took only one quick glance at the appropriate place to ascertain that it had not been fired. She felt relief of sorts—and passed the gun over to Took to hold. Took obviously had a look at it as well, because her face looked markedly more relaxed. There was still doubt in Took's eyes, though—doubt mirrored in her own heart.

"What next now that our boys have fled the course?" asked Ted, brightening a bit.

"Surely we have enough now."

"No," said Jane, shaking her head. "We're going back to their quarters and have a peek in. I have a hunch that there's one more bit of this business that we should record"—she patted her machinery as though it were some sort of talisman—"before we flee."

Took looked up doubtfully to the horizon, which had darkened immensely.

"I don't know if we're going to be able to leave even if we want to," she said, voice grave.

Jane looked again at the approaching storm.

The darkness seemed to deepen even as she watched, moving like a huge, living, black thing, clawing its way across the sky.

CHAPTER

When Liz Brogan had
been very young, a long, long time ago (or at
least it *seemed* a very long time ago), she had
been a fearless little girl. Stubborn, willful,
defiant of all normal forms of domestic danger
such as heights, cars, cats, dogs, electrical sockets, mothers, fathers, and older brothers, she
had been the wonder and bane of her protective
parents.

The one exception, the one area that bothered her, even from before true consciousness
set it, was the dark. She always needed a night-
light, she avoided dark alleys at night, the horror movies that she had the hardest time with
involved darkness and night. It was always as
though, she realized, the lack of light created
an imbalance with the rest of her faculties,

including a faintly psychic one, sensitive to the ominous motions and denizens that darkness could hold.

Liz was afraid of the dark.

When he was in a particularly sadistic phase of his malevolent boyhood (or so it seemed to her), her brother would sometimes pull out her night-light and wake her up. Her parents had put a stop to that pretty quickly. They'd told her that it was something that she would grow out of, something that was just a part of being a child and that when she grew tall, her head would reach far above the part of the world that was dark.

This allayed her fears somewhat then, but she still kept that night-light burning, and all the monsters of the galaxy seemed to lurk in her stygian closet.

So when the lights went out in that Tarn chamber—a chamber that felt more like a tomb or sepulcher than a simple analysis tech shop or whatever it claimed to be, Liz Brogan braced herself for the terror she expected to pour in at any moment.

Nothing, however, happened.

She was unmoved.

She was in total darkness in the midst of an alien place, but she felt no fear. She knew, within a very short time, that this was for other reasons: she felt *other* things in the chamber with them, and they did not induce anything but simple curiosity and openness—no, not things . . . not things at all but rather presences, *benign* presences, standing just beyond them, not approaching, and most certainly not threatening.

This was not the most astonishing thing, though. That would be the reaction of Matt.

"Don't worry, Liz," he said. She heard the sounds of Matt fishing through the junk in his pocket. "I've got an omni-light somewhere."

"Quick!" cried Orrin, his teeth literally chattering with terror. "Get it on. This is awful."

There was a clattering as Matt fumbled out his light and tried to turn it on.

"Damn. Something's wrong with the battery. Nothing's happening," said Matt, and although Liz appreciated his concern for her, she nonetheless relished the fright that was in his voice, especially since she knew that everything was all right, everything was in fact just fine.

She was about to tell him just that when another voice from beyond them spoke instead, beating her to the punch.

"Fear not," it said. "Merely a necessary test." The voice was smooth and silky and reassuring and definitely female. "The absence of light always aids us in predetermining your psychic nature and any possible harm you might intend. We are quite happy to meet and work with you. Welcome."

Slowly, reassuringly, light returned.

Orrin and Matt seemed to take the speaker's words to heart, because there was no scramble for the door. They simply stood and watched as the lights commenced to illuminate the tall, slender figure standing immediately before them, holding out robed arms as though invoking spirits beyond their understanding.

"You have something for me, I believe," said the Tarn before them, staring with a mixture of curiosity and businesslike calm at the new arrivals. "Janar called before you."

"You are S'nath?" said Matt.

"Yes, I am that personage . . . Now then, I am a busy woman. Please let's be about our business. Show the soul-jewel. It is most curious for one to be abandoned. This does not bode well. No, not at all."

Liz looked back at Orrin and Matt. They were just standing there like statues, looking absolutely stunned at the authoritarian figure standing before them. She, however, felt oddly comforted. This person was clearly in charge. Liz could sense that, and more as well: knowledge, wisdom, deep spirituality.

She pulled out the thing that she had found in the park and, reverently, tendered it.

In the palm of her hand, the soul-jewel glittered and glowed with a preternatural aura, looking like something whipped up in a special effects film lab. The previously cold thing also felt faintly warm in her palm . . . no, it was growing even hotter as she passed the thing over to the mistress of this domain.

The Tarn woman, she could see now, had deep glowing eyes within the confines of the twin falls of silver hair. The third eye in the middle of her forehead was opening and it gleamed, resplendent with an emerald sheen.

S'nath plucked the jewel from Liz's palm and brought it up to her forehead, alongside the third eye.

Her other eyes lowered and the lower part of her face wrinkled with a frown.

"Hmmm," she said. "Most alarming. It is well that you have brought this here."

With a swoosh of robes and the faint scent of lavender, she was gone, taking the jewel off to the side of the room. A touch of fingernail to the wall brought forth the whir of internal machinery. Servomotors sounded and shelves with lumps and clumps of elaborate alien items extruded. It all looked suddenly like the laboratory of some extraterrestrial alchemist.

Liz took a sudden breath, almost a gasp, as the realization sank in: in a way, it was just that.

"Amazing," whispered Matt to Orrin. "Looks to me like we came to the right place. Thanks."

"Yeah," whispered Orrin, eyes wide with awe. "No problem."

S'nath hit a button. A tray extended from a lumpish boulder thing. The Tarn placed the soul-jewel upon the tray, waved a hand over it—almost like some ornate magician in the midst of an elaborate trick—and the tray withdrew.

Immediately there were deep, soft internal chimes within the array. Clinkings and musical clankings. Lights bright and soft appeared upon the face of the instrumentation. A sour citrus smell emerged.

"What's going on?" asked Matt.

"Haven't the faintest," returned Orrin.

"Shhh!" said Liz. It was almost as though her own concentration upon this was an extremely important component.

A spectrum of lights washed over the ceiling, twirling colorfully and somberly. The Tarn psychic scientist touched the machine thoughtfully, then turned to her visitors.

"It will be a moment," she said. "I assume my associates have informed you of the importance and nature of what you have brought to me?"

"Yes," said Liz.

S'nath grunted. "It is very odd for one of these to be found upon a field." She gestured toward the vague closeness. "We store them here, you know. In the Collective."

"Yes. Racial memory," piped Matt the know-it-all.

He received a stern look from the Tarn psychic scientist. "Hardly the proper term. You Earth people can be so arrogant. You believe you know so much. You should be open to the depths of experience that other unused portions of the brain can give you. Young male, you should emulate your sister more."

Liz wanted to turn and stick out her tongue at her brother. The gesture, however, hardly seemed appropriate now. In fact, she was totally swept up in the proceedings here: it was as though, suddenly, she was much older and wiser. She wasn't sure she liked the feeling, but she accepted it without question.

"You know the identity of the owner of this soul-jewel?" asked Orrin, returning to his role of investigating policeman and clearly finding comfort in it.

"The soul-jewel is presently being analyzed for the exact answer to that question, Officer," said S'nath. "But I can tell you from my own observations that the individual was murdered . . . And since we have a record of those dead whose jewels we have not yet received, I have a very strong suspicion of who the Tarn is—"

"Or was," said Matt.

"One never speaks of a Tarn in the past tense," pronounced the woman in ominous tones. "For while individuality may recess, its essence still remains imprinted in History and in the All."

Liz's eyes were wide, taking it all in. It was a deliciously melodramatic chapter of her life and she was enjoying it immensely. However, now she was getting a discordant sensation. There was something else going on that could be of immense importance to her and to those she loved:

She felt trepidation.

A screen appeared, warping and wrapping itself around reality and image: lights flashed with angry color. Images flew across the display.

A keyboard popped up before S'nath, and her fingers played over it deftly.

She grimaced as she did so.

"I'm damping this down to all but the visual. There's a large amount here that could be very painful to any of you with any kind of empathic powers."

Twinges: Liz felt some of that pain, hinted at, like the faint jabs of pain one felt when anesthetized in the dentist's office.

The entirety of the machine array reconfigured. The images flashed quickly. So quickly that Liz could not quite interpret their meaning.

"These are the images—snapshots, if you will," said S'nath, "that are recorded from the Tarn individual onto his soul-jewel. I am presently cross-referencing the material here with the information on our computers to receive some kind of fix on the identity and—"

The Tarn stopped in mid-sentence.

Her face, previously stoic, suddenly changed to one filled with alarm.

"What's wrong?" asked Matt.

"Yeah. You don't need psychic powers to see that somethin's eating at ya," added Orrin.

"Amazing. Oww . . ." The Tarn put a hand to her head, as though fending off a headache of splitting proportions. "Owwww!" Quickly another hand reached out and flung a switch on full. S'nath cringed as though she had just received a blast full of pure pain.

Liz didn't know what to do. However, a moment later, the Tarn stood up and seemed to be back in charge of her faculties.

"This," she said, "is something I had not expected at all."

"No kiddin'," said Orrin. "You wanna start fillin' us in. You're talkin' to a police officer here."

"And a police lieutenant's kids . . ."

"Yes, yes . . ." said S'nath. "Lieutenant Patrick Brogan. I have seen him in the vision."

"Vision. What are you talking about?" said Liz.

"Also: a partner. Yes. Psychic resonances indicate . . . let me cross-reference"—a finger to her head—"an Officer Haldane, I believe."

"Yes! That would be Jack!" said Liz. "Please, S'nath. Tell us what's going on!"

The Tarn psychic analysis specialist turned to them and looked at them with grave import. "I'm afraid," she said, "your father, your friend—and other males associated with them—are even as we speak, in great peril."

CHAPTER

Thunder rolled.

It shook the building, wracking the rafters, with a hefty crack and a curious shivery echo to the sweep of lightning illumination that had just washed through the large antechamber of the Brotherhood's lodge.

Something in Jack Haldane shivered deeply as he looked around at his companions, standing in readiness for what awaited them.

There was Podly, decked out in a curious spiky hunting armor, looking like a lonely porcupine. And there, beside him, was Cradla, in a similar outfit, holding a large energy rifle that looked more like an intricately carved harpoon gun. Colors and shadows glittered in its bowels. Beside them, looking decidedly uncomfortable in reduced armor was Patrick Brogan. He had chosen a more standard Earth-style rifle, exactly as Haldane had chosen.

All in all, Jack Haldane felt like a doomed Anglo-Saxon about to go ahunting for Grendel's mother.

He just wished Beowulf was around to give them a boost, a song—and maybe a flagon of mead.

Rain pattered on the roof outside.

"Uhm, Captain," said Jack, finally summoning up the nerve to speak his mind. "Do you really think this is wise? I mean, going out into that storm."

Podly gave him an acid look. "That's not just any storm, Haldane."

"Aye," said Cradla, looking strong and dour. His eyes seemed huge and piercing, like twin portholes into a crystalline Valhalla. "It's the *morgath*."

It was nasty, all right. Haldane had read about the titans of Altorian weather. They were like Earth storms in that they were violent with huge winds and much whipping about of water and power. However, because of the curious meteorological conditions here on Altor, odd electrical things happened within the upper portions of the storms, rendering travel through them by air highly dangerous. The transmission of any kinds of radio waves through this barrier, be they sophisticated or simple, was absolutely impossible.

In short, here on Dreek Island, they were cut off from the outside world.

No. Strike that, thought Jack Haldane.

The outside *Universe.*

"Well, we're just doing our best to fit in, I suppose," said Brogan with an expulsion of breath. "But I can't help but wonder why we can't go hunting while the sun is up." He peered out through the window. Beyond was darkness and the scream of wind. "It looks pretty rough out there."

Podly walked to the window, took a quick gaze out, snorted. "Pah. It's nothing. We've gone hunting in far worse weather." He smiled, and his big eyes gleamed. "Besides, if the weather's a little worse than usual—why, that just puts a little more challenge into the equation, eh?"

Behind them, the rest of the males on Dreek Island raised their cups of drink and cried out strong affirmatives.

Of course, noted Haldane, they were all comfortably attired and enjoying their eating and drinking. No armor on *them*. They had no intention or need of going out into the jungle, looking for some sort of strange wild beast in the midst of a storm. They could just sit in here comfortably on their alien butts and applaud all they cared to because they were going to stay dry and warm while the new guys and a couple of the old went out and got drenched while risking their necks in the name of manhood.

No, not even *man*hood. *Male*hood.

Haldane suddenly saw it all.

Saw the cause of grief and evil and suffering through the Universe. He realized his own life in context. His experiences with the police force on Earth—no, with the whole group of men that he'd dealt with from his father and brothers on down through school, sports, Boy Scouts, and all the other nonsensical gatherings he'd been involved with.

What it all was some kind of crazy form of psychobiology. For some reason males were always in some sort of competition, whether it be over food, females, money, or what have you. The only thing they cared to celebrate was that competition among themselves, and that was their commonality. And if they got the chance, to see other males competing and making fools of themselves in some sort of tribal rites.

Well, it was okay when he was a teenager and okay when he was a cop back on Earth. He'd been immersed in it all then. But taken out of context and put in this situation—a situation where he was in silly armor with a silly gun and supposed to go out into a serious storm searching for snipes with fangs . . .

Well, it was time to get out of alien Boy Scouts.

He thought about pleading a headache or intestinal distress, but he knew that just wouldn't work.

He'd have to plead the truth.

"You know what, Captain Podly," he said. "You put me down on Demeter City and tell me to go get a criminal or save a family—or anything that's my duty as a cop, and I'll do it." He folded his arms together and affected a stern stand. "I'm sorry, but in my humble opinion, this hunting business—and hunting like this on a day that's not fit for man or beast—is something that's not at all in my line of duty."

He could see Patrick Brogan's eyes widen, first with astonishment, then flare with anger. Jack knew this alien bonding business was important to him, but you could only take things so far. Sure, Jack Haldane was happy to get to know other creatures. But not at the expense of his humanity, his dignity—and hey, maybe his life as well.

"Jack—" said Brogan.

"I'm sorry," said Haldane. "All this . . . I mean, it's just stupid and suicidal. Risking your neck in the streets is one thing. Hell, Lieutenant . . . *and* Captain. I'll lay my life on the line for any one of you . . . and for my job. That's pretty much all wrapped up in the oath I took as a cop." He gently set his power rifle up against the wall. "This, though, has nothing to do with any of that. I respect your customs, and I'm sure they all have a purpose, Captain Podly. Seems to me, though, customs have to get examined and reevaluated from time to time."

Podly looked as though he was about to blow a gasket. For a moment, his face was a sunset red. However, he let out a breath . . . and stepped toward Haldane.

He raised a hand and for a moment Haldane thought he was going to get slapped. He almost flinched, but he stood firm.

Instead of a slap, though, Podly patted his officer on the shoulder. "Good fellow. You have a very good argument," said the captain. He looked over the group of other Creons and Tarns in attendance. "He's right you know. Never doubt it. This is a good being here, and a good cop. He's young and cocky sometimes, but he'll come through in a pinch. You should respect him even though he seems to be backing out of this challenge."

Haldane stiffened, feeling a little odd, but maintaining his stance. "Thanks, Captain."

"It will be your human comrade, then, that will reap all the glory," said Podly.

Brogan had looked as though he was about to join the mutiny. But now that Podly had put the situation to him in those terms, how could he.

Haldane felt *very* bad. But what could he do?

Besides, he wasn't merely taking the correct line, he was taking the safe line.

"Yes. That's right," said Brogan, grudgingly. "I get to hog all the honors."

Haldane hoped that Podly didn't get the sarcasm in his partner's voice.

"Tell you what," he said. "I'll keep my armor and my arms. You guys get in trouble out there"—he tapped his plated chest—"I'll come out and save you. That's something you can count on. The rest of this stuff—well, it's just against my religion, I guess."

Podly made a dismissive gesture, then wrapped a fatherly arm around the young officer. "No problem, m'boy. Absolutely no problem whatsoever." He gestured toward the assembled party. "There are other activities of an affiliating nature available here for you with our comrades. True, my friends. Games, song, wine—but no women."

"You're not going to cross-dress tonight?" asked Haldane, hopefully.

Podly raised a scraggly eyebrow. "What! Of course not! That is a first night activity!"

"Games galore await, however," promised a piping, somewhat slurred voice.

Podly poked his subofficer's chest. "And you will hopefully join in with full enthusiasm."

Haldane gulped. What the hell was in store? He wondered if that was why Podly was not particularly upset about his staying at the compound.

Was something *worse* awaiting him here?

Oh well. At least he was going to stay dry.

"Fine. I'm ready for anything that doesn't involve chasing crazed fierce animals."

The assembly held up their mugs and cheered.

Podly left and spoke in low tones to Cradla as they put their gear together.

Brogan sidled over to Haldane as he started to take off his clanking armor. "You know, I think old Podly actually respects your decision."

"I don't know about that, Pat. I'm just not a hunter, I guess. Golf and cross-dressing were okay. Gotta draw the line somewhere, though."

"I wouldn't have thought it, but your stand, your statement of values, seems to have their respect. Of course it leaves me in the lurch . . . but then, I'm the senior officer." Brogan scratched his nose. "I suppose that's my job."

"Look, I meant it about calling for help."

"The long-range radio's not working because of the storm," said Brogan.

"Short-range is, buddy," said Haldane. "Do you think I would have volunteered to come if I didn't know that? I'm not going to let you go off with a bunch of strangers unless I'm absolutely sure that you're going to be able to call me, so I can save your butt."

Brogan clapped him on the shoulder. "I didn't doubt you for a moment, friend."

"More like a minute, huh?"

"Yeah. Something like that."

They shared a laugh, and Jack felt good.

There was a lot of strange stuff that had happened to him here on Altor. Much of it he had mixed feelings about. However, he had absolutely no doubt that what had gone on between him and his friend and partner, hell almost *brother* now, was all good.

"Yeah. Well, I guess you'd better get on out there and get that thing—whatever it is they want you to get," said Haldane.

Brogan looked contemplative.

"Something wrong?" asked Haldane.

"That Cradla. Does he bother you?"

"Yeah. Still, we've already heard—he's a rival of Podly, who got beat out by the captain. Bound to be a little bit jealous."

"Yeah, well, I don't like the idea of him and us being out alone out there in a storm with power weapons."

Haldane thought about this for a moment. Come to think of it, he didn't like it much, either.

"Shit. You want me to come too, man? Just in case."

"No. Podly's a big boy. He can take care of himself. No, actually, it's all for the good if you stay here, come to think of it."

"Why's that?"

Brogan smiled. "Like you said, so you can come and save our butts."

"Count on it."

Brogan gave him a thumbs-up and went back to the hunting group.

Haldane looked over to the partying Creons and Tarns, wondering if maybe Brogan didn't have the better end of the bargain.

CHAPTER

"By the wounds of the
great God Index," said Orrin, "however did I get
talked into this?"

The knuckles of his big hands were white upon
the wheel of the hopper.

And for very good reason: the vehicle was over a
large stretch of white-topped water, shaking and
shivory like a frightened animal. A spatter of rain
and slap of wind. A melodramatic stream of lightning and the answering growl of thunder—they
were descending into the storm.

Liz could smell the fear in the air, and realized
that part of it was hers. But then, there was nothing
else to do. They had to get down there, they *had* to
reach Dreek Island. It was a matter of life and death.

And the most precious life involved was her
father's.

"You're here because there's no other choice," said Liz.

Orrin knew that. Just as well as Liz and Matt knew it. They'd all made the decision together. Now, though, doubtlessly Orrin was complaining to let off steam at a time of stress.

The situation had been clear-cut, simple.

Even as Liz thought about it, the scene slipped back into her head, almost superimposed over the storm.

"Danger?" she had said to S'nath in the Collective.

The woman's third eye seemed to tremble, shudder in its place in her forehead. It seemed slightly protruding, bloodshot, as though it had just gone through an ordeal and was even now enduring something rigorously unpleasant. There was the smell of charcoal and damp besides the jasmine incense—the scent of distant fires.

"To loved ones?" repeated Matt, without a trace of sarcasm. He looked pale, and clearly felt not at all in his usual control of the situation.

Orrin opened his mouth to say something but, wide-eyed, could only flap his jaws. A tiny squeak emerged from his mouth. In normal police procedure, Liz had no doubt that Orrin could operate quite efficiently. However, everything about this place and situation smacked of abnormality. And, if not the supernatural, then at least on the very tippy end of "natural" at least.

"Let me explain," said S'nath. "No. Allow me to illustrate."

The Tarn, with a swirling of robes, swept up to the bizarre and intricate contraption that had previously been flashing confused and juxtaposed images of the deceased Tarn's life. Now, though, all that remained was a twisted chiaroscuro of lines and jagged color, an abstract artwork fluctuating between meaningless chaos and vertiginous revelation.

It seemed pregnant with meaning to Liz. And yet, the meaning was so obtuse and oblique it might as well have been nonsense. Only this Tarn could translate, she realized, and now that she was passing wrinkled fingers over quivering bulbs, she seemed to be doing just that.

"Look," said the Tarn portentously. "Look deeply into the warp screen."

"I don't see a thing," said Matt, squinting and turning his head this way and that, as though catching the view from some different angle would make a difference.

"Nonsense," pronounced Orrin. "There's nothing there to see."

Tarn fingers twitched. Fine-tuned.

Slowly, something came into focus on the screen. An image.

"I'm starting to make something out!" said Liz.

Slowly angles and lines were converging with contour and form to produce a recognizable picture.

It seemed to be a view of a large gothic-cum-rococo skyscraper, centered upon one of the topmost of its levels.

"The last moment of full vision of the recently

assassinated businessman, Zin Mooka," said S'nath in soft but fluid tones. "Perhaps the very moment the bullet expertly impacted upon his life, cutting it down."

Matt pointed excitedly. "Look—I see a rifle sticking out up there."

She could see it!

"Can you zoom in?" asked Liz, excitedly.

"Yes."

The picture changed, pushing in and expanding on the contents of its center.

That central image was magnified.

"I'm making out features," said Matt.

"It's a man with a gun," said Liz. "The assassin. We can figure out his identity."

"Not necessarily," said Orrin. "He could easily have utilized some kind of alter-tech to—" The Creon stopped in mid-sentence, stepped forward, looking stunned. He extended a thick forefinger, pointed it toward the man in the picture. "I've seen that guy!"

Liz and Matt swung their heads toward the Creon, astonished.

Only S'nath seemed not to be surprised.

"Who is it?" said Matt.

"Have you got a name?" asked Liz.

"I don't know about a name . . . can't quite remember . . . but the man definitely. And he stopped in the precinct to see Officer Castle."

"Jane Castle?" asked Liz.

"Yes. I remember it definitely. Yes—his name was Ted Something. . . . Ted Bickford, I think."

"Jane Castle has a friend who's an assassin," said Matt, trying to take it all in.

Orrin's face underwent an aggrieved change of expression.

"What's wrong, Orrin?" demanded Liz.

"You know something, Orrin. We can tell. Cough it up," said Matt.

"I can't . . . I promised . . . Oh dear . . . She'll hang me from the docking bay by my tongue—She'll . . ."

The Tarn named S'nath directed a strong, piercing gaze at the Creon. "You may as well tell. I have long since extracted your secret. It is intertwined in my assessment of the danger present in the situation now."

"Spill it, Orrin," said Matt.

"Orrin, if it involves danger to our loved ones," said Liz, "you'd better tell us."

Orrin nodded solemnly. "Yes. I must. She would want me to. Poor Jane." He sighed heavily. "When this man—this Ted Bickford—came in, I happened to overhear their plans."

"Plans?" said Matt. "Jane Castle is involved with an assassin's plans to kill someone?"

Orrin shook his head emphatically. "No, no, nothing at all like that. Apparently, Jane Castle was very upset at not being invited to Dreek Island."

"Was that the training place where Dad went this week?" asked Liz, putting two and two together.

"Yes, exactly," continued Orrin. "Jane was clearly quite angry that females were excluded from the happenings, you know."

"Excluded!" said Liz. "And well she should be upset." She looked over to S'nath for a gesture of solidarity, but received only a blank look.

"Yeah, well, bustin' up the fun didn't sit right with me, but Jane's a friend and she convinced me I shouldn't squeal, that all she was after was equality." Orrin raised his hands in a resigned gesture. "So everybody gets to go to Dreek Island but me!"

That got an odd look from S'nath.

"But you say that this . . . this assassin was visiting her?" asked Liz.

"Yes, and it seemed perfectly fine with me because I'd met him a couple of years ago when they seemed to be dating," said Orrin. "At least that was the word that Jane used."

"Jane was dating an assassin?" Matt shook his head in disbelief. "I can't believe it."

"You must realize that although the average Tarn's psi powers are limited, mine are larger—and amplified by my link with the collective," said S'nath abruptly. "My psychic sources confirm this information, which I previously gleaned from this Creon's mind. And this is why I say that a loved one is in danger: for, from all indications, it would seem that this is no holiday this human killer is taking, nor merely is it so that he can aid Jane Castle in her unusual mission."

She lapsed into silence, closed her eyes, and held up her hand to the machine.

"So tell us already," demanded Liz. "If my father's in danger, tell us why."

Slowly, the Tarn opened her eyes.

They had changed color to the darkest of dramatic blues. "Your father has made enemies on Demeter City."

"That's part of his job," said Matt. "He's a cop."

"This assassin, Ted Bickford," said S'nath with immense finality, "has apparently received orders to kill a high-ranking officer on Dreek Island."

Why on Dreek Island, Liz wondered again as she looked at the swirls of weather lashing all about them violently as they made their way through the storm. Why not some other more accessible place. That was truly a puzzle. But they hadn't had time to sort it out or wonder much.

Time was of the essence.

They had to warn their dad! It could be him the guy was after!

Unfortunately, by the time they'd exited the Collective, the storm had its grip not only upon Dreek Island but Demeter City as well. Communication to the island, much less to the Station House in Precinct 88, was impossible.

They had the hopper they'd used to come down to the Tarn Collective. They had no choice but to get in it and make their way through the storm.

They had to either stop this assassin, or somehow warn Jane Castle or their father.

Hence this mad journey.

"Look!" cried Matt, peering through the rain-streaked window. "Is that it down there?"

Liz looked as Orrin responded. "Yes! According to the navigational programs, that should indeed be the place."

Through the madness of wind and rain, a faint clearing had come, showing a craggy bit of earth, against which waves bashed madly.

"Take her down," said Liz.

Orrin twisted the controls, and slowly the hopper tilted downward to the island below.

Liz just prayed they would arrive in time.

Whatever is going on down there now? she wondered.

CHAPTER

Jane Castle watched
as the hunting party made its way out the gates,
into the lashing wind and the rain. One of its ten
members was playing some kind of song on a toot-
ing instrument. *No, it can't be,* she thought, hun-
kering down lower in her protective sheath of
raingear.

"Colonel Bogey's March"?

No. Surely not.

The weather was yelling at the top of its lungs
all around them. King Lear time. Oh boy. She was
trying to get this crazy little march into whatever
down for posterity, using her recording equipment,
but she wasn't at all sure what the hell was actually getting impressed inside.

"What do you think?" she said, above the howl
howl howl of the elements.

"I told you what I think before, and it's still exactly the same," said Took. "I think we should go back to the hopper where it's safe and warm and dry, bundle up tight, have a nap, and wait out this storm. Then we should go back home before we get caught. We've done all we can here."

Jane half agreed.

However, there was something bothering her, something that nagged at the back of her mind about what was going on. Partly, she thought that there was more to record, more to buttress her argument for eradication of the barriers between males and females in the police ranks.

Something more, though . . .

Some gut feeling niggling inside of her, telling her that her presence was needed for some other reason. What it was she had absolutely no idea. But still, with these two factors weighing heavily, she could hardly bury her head in the sand of the distant hopper, dry though it might be.

"No," she said. "What I mean is, what do you think—should we follow that party and film—or go down to the compound and see what's going on there?" She turned to the man of the team for his opinion.

"I get a say?" he asked, surprised. "What if I agree with Took and say snuggle up inside the hopper till this storm blows over?" Rain was dribbling down his face and he didn't look particularly comfortable.

"That's not an option, I'm afraid."

"Okay. Well, it's obvious that the truly interesting stuff is going on with that hunting party. Frankly, though, the idea of following a hunting party whose sole intent is to blow the head off of anything that moves seems like a pretty stupid idea to me. You seem to be intent upon the idea of filming whatever's going on inside the compound. Chances are we can be a lot drier and a lot safer inside that compound than out here. So, that's where my vote is to go!"

Jane looked at him.

Poor guy looked like a drowned rat, with a queasy appealing smile pasted on his pale face. What he certainly did not look like was any kind of threat. Any paranoia she was feeling seemed to just peel away.

"I must say, that sounds like the best choice to me," said Took, her voice watery.

"Any kind of psychic predictions?"

"Sorry. Doesn't work that way I'm afraid. Rationally, though, I can't argue with our friend's diagnosis of the situation. So I guess it's back to the compound."

They watched the party of hunters traipse off into the wilds, exotic tips of exotic weapons pointing off to the blackened sky, danger, mystery, and total lunacy.

What made males do these kinds of things? she wondered. It all seemed a total enigma to her, perhaps as mysterious as life itself if certainly not nearly so profound. Was it some odd inner organ located somewhere in the prehistoric R-complex that injected them with needs and drives beyond the comprehension of sane beings (i.e., females). Or was it the engines of culture and survival, competition and psychobiology?

In any case, whatever the curious mix of chemical and psychological realities, Jane Castle was right in the middle of the stew. Not only was it her commitment to paddle about gamely, but to make it a better stew for those of her sex throughout the system.

For while the male processes seemed a puzzling mass of metaphors clashing with one another, it was Jane Castle's duty as a female to introduce equality into that mass, and then mix those metaphors properly!

Yes!

Even now, in the midst of rainy misery, she saw her purpose bright and steadfast before her. Indeed, narrating these shocking exposures of male custom and insularity that she was obtaining on her recorder, she would go down in feminist history as the first to strike a blow for *intergalactic* equality.

Yesterday was the era of the suffragettes.

Tomorrow was her time.

For she, Jane Castle, would surely be known as a suffra-*jet*!

With this vision and goal bolstering and fortifying her resolve, Jane waited for the last of the hunters to disappear into the rainy mist, and then she gestured her people onward toward the last stretch of the road toward Victory.

In the storm, the compound seemed to have let down its guard. There were no signs of sentries, alive or electric. The battlements were easy to scale. In fact, all Jane and company had to do was to walk through the open gates.

Well, skulk actually.

Jane took them against the wall, blending in with the darkness and gloom, the mist and the wet.

She could smell the warmth inside, taste the good cheer. However, she held herself back from rushing forward. It was best not to get too cocky and confident. Caution was the best component of their effort at this point.

Through the storm strained the sound of muted song.

"My, my," said Took ironically. "Sounds like more nefarious male bonding and shenanigans."

"We don't know what's going until we have a look." Jane pointed down an alleyway. "That's where we were last night. Sounds as though the shocking ceremonies are occurring in exactly the same place."

"That's where we'll have to go then, isn't it?" said Ted Bickford, seemingly totally accepting of Jane's dictates.

Jane appreciated the support. "Very quietly, though. It's daytime and they might not be so drunk and unaware of our presence." She looked up and gauged the lie of the land. "Also, I should think that even though it is raining, we should keep to the shadows, as it were." She pointed.

"Under that roofing over there. We'll sidle along carefully, making sure that there's no one about."

A simple plan, and a good one.

Also, a comparatively dry one: there was a roof of sorts overhanging the walkway.

Even though the storm in the sky was making all sorts of fuss, they moved over to the walkway every bit as quietly as they had the last time, slinking, skulking, low to the ground as they could go. The weather seemed to warp and crack and shout above them, wracking and wringing the land and the sky. It had an odd smell to it, this storm, a different kind of taste and feel. There was an electricity to it that was of a different nature and character than the thundershowers that Jane had experienced on Earth. There was ozone in the mix, yes—but other, more ominous chemicals as well.

Perhaps even a touch of sulfur.

Underneath the awning was immediate relief, and a change in volume. Jane no longer felt as though she was stuck in the middle of a huge bass drum.

"Whew!" she whispered. "I think you two have definitely made the correct call. I don't know how Haldane and Brogan are going to be able to deal with all that with that hunting armor on."

"Maybe the armor is engineered for such storms," suggested Bickford. "That *could* be why they're wearing it."

Jane hadn't thought of that. "I know you're an engineer, but I didn't know you had that kind of mind."

Bickford shrugged. "Just adding two and two. When it's hot out, you wear shorts. When it's raining, you put on your galoshes. When it's storming and you've got to shoot large creatures—well—strikes me that you've got to use something a little stronger." He looked thoughtful, as though he was just working some of these things out in his own mind.

"That's all well and good," said Took, still in a low voice. "But just the same, *I* wouldn't like to be stuck in one of those suits in the middle of an alien island!"

Jane was taken aback. "But Took . . . Surely this island isn't alien to you. Altor is your home."

"You forget, Jane—Altor is an adopted home," said the Tarn softly. "Much of it is as strange to me as it is to you. This island, to me, is alien."

Jane considered that a moment. Yes, even back home in New Europe, sometimes she felt like a stranger. Sometimes she felt like an alien in the midst of the things that were most familiar. That was why it was so easy to volunteer to come here to a different world as soon as the opportunity came up.

"Fascinating," said Bickford. "You said similar things to me while we were getting to know each other, Jane."

"I did?" she said. She'd forgotten how close she'd gotten to the man—even when she barely knew him. There must have been a great need for intimacy in that frightened young woman back then—a need she'd somehow managed to close off now.

"You did indeed. One of the many reasons I couldn't help but come back to see you, Jane. That was why I was hoping that we could become close again. That's why I'm here . . . to regain your trust. To help you, to earn your forgiveness."

Jane blushed. "Please, Ted. This hardly seems the time. Besides, Took's here."

"Does that really make a difference? She's psychic. Besides, surely somebody doesn't have to be psychic to see how I feel about you."

Took's eyes were enormous in the gloom. However, her central third eye was clamped shut. "Please, don't involve me in all this. My powers are limited in both spheres."

"Ted, perhaps we can discuss this subject at some later time," suggested Jane. "There's a job to be done here. When we get back, we'll discuss these things, all right?"

"Sure. Just saw an open door. Just sticking my foot in. Hope I didn't stick it in my mouth."

Jane smiled. "No, Ted. We'll talk. It's just a very inopportune time, as I said."

"Okay, okay. Glad to get your attention though." Ted Bickford smiled as well, and a warm glow spread through her heart, despite herself.

She signaled for silence and then they edged along the building. There was the corner that they had to turn to get to the perch they had occupied before . . .

Jane Castle went first.

And bumped directly into Jack Haldane.

◆　　◆　　◆

"Officer Castle!"

"Jack!"

"Ah. . . . Jane!"

"Uhm. . . . Jack!"

"Jane Castle!"

"Jack, what are you doing here?"

She said it indignantly, hand on the hip of her slicker. She was dripping rain and looking for all the world like a drowned goddess.

"Hey! That's my question. I was *invited* here." He looked over at her companions. "Took . . . You're not supposed to be here either." He looked at Ted Bickford. "And you! Who *are* you, anyway?"

"Just call me Ted," said the man, a winning hail-and-well-met smile upon his face. "Ted Bickford." He extended a hand. Haldane was unable to do anything else but shake that hand. "Glad to meet you. It's all my fault, really. I'd heard about this island and wanted to get a look at it. I'm afraid I persuaded my friend Jane to bring me here. Officer Took came along to help on the tour, kind soul that she is."

"Ted, that's thoughtful of you to try and cover, but it's really not necessary," Jane turned and faced Jack Haldane. There was the fire of defiance in her eyes. It gave Jack an odd, visceral thrill. "We're here, Jack, to uncover the activities that occur on this island. The segregation of male and female in the Demeter City Police Force is an antediluvian practice that is patently unfair. I mean to bring it out to galactic attention so that my grievances against it can be considered well and thoughtfully by the populace at large!"

Jack stared at her, still stunned. His gaze drifted down toward the equipment that Ted Bickford held.

"That's a camera!" he found himself saying.

"Yes, that's what it is," said Jane, in a clipped, no-nonsense manner.

"How l-l-long . . ." Jack stuttered, the realization emerging like an overbearing monster from the horizon. "How long have you been here?"

"Since yesterday," said Jane.

"You . . . recorded . . . last . . . night . . . ?"

"Yes."

The images of the antics and bizarre rites of yesterday evening flashed through Jack's mind. Then they narrowed and were inserted into a vid picture . . .

Flashed throughout the Known Universe.

"Oh my God," he said. "Look, Jane. All this is not my fault. Brogan and I . . . Well, Podly *made* us come."

"Yes. Right. Absolutely."

"You don't believe me?"

"I think that, in the hearts of most males, there is a bit that thrills at the exclusion of females," said Jane.

"I'm not going to argue fine points," said Haldane, feeling desperation sink its nasty teeth into his throat. "But you've got to believe me . . . I'm not really enjoying myself here, and neither is Patrick. But who are we to rock the boat of alien customs. You're putting us between a rock and a hard place, Jane." He looked back fearfully at the main hall. "I was just out getting some fresh air here, folks. But if those guys find you here, there's going to be hell to pay."

"What's going on in there?" Jane asked. "We demand to know. Some other odd male tribal rites?"

"Actually, believe it or not, nothing like last night. Just very tame versions of cards and dominoes . . ." said Jack. "Look, Jane, you're probably right about the inequality here . . . But is this really the wise way of doing it?"

"It's the immediate and the effective way, Jack," said Jane, standing firm on her principles and position. "Are you with us . . . or against us?"

"With you, I guess. I've about had it with stupidity, vital alien male bonding or no."

"Officer Haldane," called a voice. "Where are you?"

Jack looked back at the source of the voice, and heard the pounding of footsteps coming toward them.

He had to hide these interlopers, or there would be alien hell to pay.

But the question was: where?

CHAPTER

Patrick Brogan's supposedly watertight hunting armor was leaking.

He could feel the water collecting in his right boot, cold and unpleasant.

It squelched as he walked.

The rain had not let up much, but the hunters seemed unfazed by that fact. If anything, the more they walked into the obstacles created by the storm, the more bold and confident were their strides, the more arrogant the songs they sang (albeit muffled through their armor).

Two things were unfortunate about this armor that he wore. One was the fact that there were no radios inside the helmets with which to communicate. One had to yell through a tube. True, properly used, this tube actually amplified one's voice, a help in the tumbling downpour. However, it was still a pain to use, creating a great bellowing about of Creon and Tarn voices.

Any *zark* in the area could surely hear them approaching from far away.

The second unfortunate matter was the armor itself. Although they had invited humans to attend their festivities, they had clearly not anticipated this kind of storm or the need for armor. At any rate, they hadn't designed a suit especially to fit a human being and it was damned uncomfortable. Both Creons and Tarns were humanoid (or, from their point of view, humans were Creonoid or Tarnoid), so doubtless it was assumed that Earthlings would be able to fit nicely. However, when he and Jack had tried on the Tarn armor, it was too small. Only the Creon armor would work, and it was too large. Brogan, a slender guy, felt as though he was swimming in it. The helmet in particular was too large. He felt like a clapper in a bell.

So along they went, slogging through storm and wet, through fronds and rock, weapons at the ready, hunting the notorious, murderous *zark*.

"Do you smell it yet, Cradla?" barked Podly's voice through his helmet.

The big helmet of the addressed lifted up as though to sniff the wet air. "No. Nothing."

"Do you think it will be a big one?" Podly asked. "Or a truly monstrous one?"

"It shall be the prize *zark* of all time, my colleague, and we will become famous for the killing of it. Its bones shall bear witness in the trophy rooms of all our halls."

Clearly this was some sort of ritual of braggadocio, thought Brogan, although rather extremely soggy.

The whole business was a wretched affair. By now, after only fifteen minutes of travel, his whole body seemed chafed. The smell of his own rancid sweat mingled with the smell of the previous Creon occupant. And all he could taste was last night's dubious dinner and brew.

All in all, he supposed he'd rather be back there drinking fresh brew and wearing a dress.

The jungle seemed to be getting denser about them. Fortunately, there seemed to be paths through it all, and Cradla knew them. The big Creon was at the fore of the party, leading them forward through the wind and the rain and the smell of exotic flora. Up ahead, streaks of coiled alien lightning would occasionally javelin through the clouds, flashing washes of multicolored light across the craggy mountains. This lightning spit balls of itself, which would twirl around the topmost peaks of the mountains like crazy fairies aswirl in the sky.

A few minutes later, Cradla lifted an arm into the air, halting their progress.

"You sense something Cradla?" asked Podly. It was clear by the tone of his voice that the police captain was completely and totally immersed in his hunter mode. His voice had deepened and gone all melodramatic.

"I'm not—sure," replied the guide.

"What do you suggest?"

They were at a point where the path split into two parts.

One of the divergent ways dipped down into denser jungle while the other angled upward toward rockier ways.

"I think," said Cradla, "it would be best to split the party at this point." He stared down at the jungle way, considering. "The bulk of the party should continue on down this way, scouting. You, Podly, the human, Brogan, and I shall take the high road and determine locations of *zarks* suitable for hunting."

"Should we take a Tarn along for that?" asked Brogan.

Cradla sniffed. "Tarn have their own particular psychic talents. I have the talent for hunting."

Podly nodded, which did not look particularly easy in armor. "It's true. Cradla is the best hunter of the bunch. Some say he is indeed psychic—but I know the truth of the situation." Podly touched the faceplate of his helmet. "Fellow has an extraordinary sense of smell. Isn't that true, Cradla?"

The return was gruff but not without an amused tone. "I keep my secrets to myself." The helmet turned toward Podly. "So then, friend? What do you say?"

"That sounds agreeable to me," said Podly. "It will give me a wonderful opportunity to see how you work. Traveling with you is always a worthwhile lesson, Cradla."

Cradla bowed cordially. "I thank you."

"So. Are you game, Brogan?"

"I thought that was the *zark's* job."

There was much laughter at this little joke among the whole assembly.

"Very good, human," said Cradla. "You have a fine wit among you. I hope that wit makes for a good hunter."

"Proper guidance always helps," said Podly. "You can't have a better teacher in this matter than Cradla," repeated Podly. He seemed absolutely besotted with the whole affair. Seeing Podly enthusiastic about something was initially an enjoyable and pleasant change for Brogan. However, enough was enough!

"I guess the high road, while not particularly drier, has the merit of not having so much vegetable matter in the way."

"Indeed," said Cradla. "That is why it benefits us in our quest."

"Ah," was all that Brogan could think to say. He'd scored well with that last quip anyway. Best to rest on his laurels, or the Altorian equivalent.

"So then," said Podly, "it's off we go."

The other hunters howled agreement, then turned and headed off down the low path.

"I warn you, human," said Cradla. "The merriment and amusement ceases here. All the rest of the day is dead serious."

That sounded fine to Brogan. "I'm ready," he said.

The unlikely trio headed off up the angling path, alien lightning and thunder heralding their passage.

◆ ◆ ◆

"Greetings, friend Jack Haldane!" said the Creon. He rocked back and forth on the balls of his huge feet as though buffeted by some boozy phantom wind.

Jack recognized him. "Greetings, friend Xarday," he returned agreeably. "But what brings you out at such an inclement time?"

"Ah! Simply to have a good breath of foul weather—and let loose my bladder among the elements . . . Not unlike you, no?" said Xarday.

"Well, I just wanted a breath of fresh air, actually. I intend to come back inside and enjoy the rest of the celebration very soon indeed."

"Good. You are a welcome addition to our number. I must tell you there were doubters among us as to your fitness for inclusion when Captain Podly brought up your names—but you both have proved to be fine companions." The Creon belched. "Yes, and may I say you looked very fetching indeed in the garment of your world's opposite sex."

Jack gritted his teeth. "Why, yes, thank you very much. It was an honor indeed to be included."

"Now, if you would step aside, I shall be on my way to make my date with Nature."

"Uhm—gee," said Jack. "You know, Xarday, didn't I just now hear someone calling your name?"

The Creon blinked his big ungainly eyes. "What?" He cocked an ear. "I hear nothing."

"No, not now. Before you arrived. We humans have very good hearing. You must have missed it with the droning of this rain. I think they were very definitely calling you back for something particularly special . . . Couldn't quite make out the words."

"*Koshva*," said Xarday. "They were calling me back for *koshva*. But I thought that my turn for such was not to be for a few minutes yet."

"Yes, that *was* the word I heard—I think. Don't be upset if it wasn't. Look, over there, by the building." He pointed in the opposite direction. "There's a likely place for voiding."

Xarday looked at the suggested destination blearily. "Ah, yes, that *does* look like a suitable place. And then I shall go back and have my *koshva*."

"Right," said Jack. "Sounds like a terrific idea. You just go and do that."

The Creon clamped a heavy hand down on Jack's shoulder. "You're a good fellow, Jack. I don't care what the Creon women say about you."

With that, Xarday staggered off to be about his business.

"You know, Jack, he's absolutely right," said Jane. "You looked absolutely splendid in a dress."

She and the others were around the corner, up against the wall. If Jack had let the Creon by, they would have been seen. Fortunately, he'd prevented that occurrence.

"Thanks," responded Jack, assessing them. "Question is, what am I going to do with you all now."

"I know," piped Jane. "You can help us record!"

"I don't think that would be a particularly good idea, Jane. I'm not against your principles. I'm just trying to tread water, actually. Survive. Do my best."

"Oh dear. That's what all the males say. You know, if more people like my friend Ted here had the guts to step forward and *help* the cause, then things would be a lot more equal among all beings in this Universe."

Jack looked at the man.

Just who was this guy, anyway. He sensed some sort of relationship above and beyond friendship between him and Jane Castle, and he felt jealous.

Not that he and Jane had any formal, stated relationship beyond being colleagues. It was just that Jack actually wouldn't *mind* having something more—but Jane wasn't exactly totally appreciative of his efforts to achieve that intimacy. Thus there was a romantic friction between them—and, alas, poor Jack tended to get the heat from it. Heat of entirely the wrong kind.

"Well, jolly good for him. Now—how the hell did you get here?"

"A hopper."

"And where's the hopper now?"

"Hidden on the other side of the island."

"Seems to me the obvious solution is to hide yourselves along with that hopper, don't you think?" said Jack. "Then when this storm breaks, just hop along *out* of here."

"No," said Jane. "That would be entirely unacceptable."

"Why. For God's sake, Jane, if Podly catches you

here, that's going to be the end of your career. And that's the *best* thing that will happen to you."

"What, are they going to toss me in a big kettle and cook me for dinner?"

"Maybe you'll wish they had."

"That's total and utter rubbish, Jack, and you know it. We're not living in the Stone Age anymore. This is the Star Age, the era of Media and Information." She tapped her recording equipment. "And when this gets out, it will be utter power for my statement and cause."

Jack looked at Took and Bickford. Neither had the kind of fire and commitment in their eyes that Jane Castle had. Jack couldn't really read Bickford. Took just looked very weary of the whole thing.

"You know, Jane, I sympathize with your feelings, I really do. And I agree with you—going to Podly about your complaints really would not have worked."

Jane nodded, looking smug and self-righteous.

"But is this any way to work toward the progress you want? You'll just stir up bad feeling. I mean, granted both Brogan and I are not exactly having a jolly summer holiday camp experience here. But we feel we really are working toward something . . . We wouldn't be here otherwise."

"Working on something. Exactly what are you talking about, Jack? No, wait. I'll tell you. You're working on something that seems to be universal. The oppression of one sex by another. The subjugation of rights. Blatant male fascism."

"Maybe," said Jack. He let the pounding and slashing of the rain fill in the silence for a few moments, then continued. "Maybe that's true—and I guess I'm glad that's changed on Earth. But it took a hundred years, and it wasn't quite what people thought it would be, was it? I mean, it was confusing for a lot of people . . . Ah hell, I don't know what I'm saying. I'm not a sociologist. All I know is that we're not on Earth. This is an alien planet with alien ways . . . I know there are a lot of similarities, but it's still alien. Let's not anthropomorphize more than has already been done by Nature."

"What are you saying, Jack?"

"I guess I'm saying that it's taken a lot of hard work for humans to gain the trust of the Creons and the Tarns. Particularly the Creons, who don't have that psychic ability stuff. Has it occurred to you, Jane, that this little exercise might throw a monkey wrench into the works of that?"

"Rationalization," said Jane adamantly. "There is no excuse for this kind of inequality. I'm sick of it and I'm sticking to my guns, Jack. Nothing you can say can dissuade me."

"Absolutely," said Ted Bickford. "I agree with her completely. If efforts aren't started to change the Universe now, Haldane, just *when* will they start?" He cleared his throat. "In any case, before the next phase of this expedition starts, you'll have to excuse me. Nature calls. I'll just step round that building over there and be back in a jiffy." Bickford left with a toodle-oo gesture.

"Yeah, yeah," said Jack. "Just don't fall in, buddy. On second thought—"

"Jack, just because someone is more enlightened than you doesn't give you liberty to abuse him verbally," Jane said indignantly.

Jack started to say something. But the sheer uselessness of it all was overwhelming. Sunk! He and Brogan were absolutely sunk, all their efforts were for naught, unless he could get rid of Jane and company. But how? She seemed absolutely dead set on this whole business. All he could possibly hope to do was effect some kind of damage control.

Such as maybe tackling Jane and destroying whatever she was recording.

As soon as the thought entered his head, though, he nixed it. No, he simply wasn't that kind of person. Besides, for all he said, he rather agreed with Jane. She and all the women police he'd ever worked with were just as hardworking, just as valuable and smart as any man he'd ever known. This whole all-male business was absolutely ludicrous.

What was to be done, though?

"Look, Jane," he said, thinking quickly. "Let's strike a deal. You take what you've got and clear out. I think you've got pretty much what you need. When we get back, we'll have a meeting with Podly in a neutral setting. You can put forward all your points—and they do have a lot of weight, I agree—and we'll rationally deal with the situation."

"Nonsense. That sort of thing simply doesn't work!" said Jane. "Historically, it takes a different kind of force. It takes leverage. I haven't got everything I need, yet, Jack. And I think you realize that. You're trying to keep things from us, I know. For instance—just what is this *koshva* business?"

"*Koshva*? I haven't got the faintest idea, Jane."

"I think you know, and you're trying to hide another male secret from us. You just want to brush all this under the carpet, don't you? That's your style. But I won't stand for it. I call upon your humanity, Jack Haldane. You simply *have* to help us in our worthy cause."

Jack looked over to Took for help. But Took simply made a gesture of total helplessness. "I couldn't talk her out of this," said the Tarn. "She's like a force of Nature."

"No compromise then?"

Jane gave him a steely look. "No retreat. No surrender."

Jack sighed. "Okay. You're right."

Jane blinked. "I am?"

"Yes. You got me where I live, Jane. You're absolutely correct. My loyalties should be with those of my race. I have to stick to my kind. I will help disgrace my friends in the police force . . . Why? Because, as you say—they aren't human, are they? They're alien. We're human, and clearly have the right to open our big mouths and say what we like whenever we care to—because we're the greatest race in the galaxy and we must stick together, no matter what!"

A confused look came over Jane Castle's face. "Jack, I'm not doing this because I'm a racist."

"Aren't you? You're invoking my humanity as a reason to help your cause."

Jane shook her head and was silent for a moment. "Oh dear. You've managed to make the whole thing muddled where it seemed very clear before."

"Hmmm. That sounds like life to me, doesn't it, Jane? There are all kinds of sides to deal with. Now why don't you just go back to your hopper and—"

Suddenly, interrupting them, there came a wailing from the sky. A screech, a roar of rocket engines.

Jack looked up.

Angling down through the rain, buffeted by the winds, was a hopper. It looked to be in trouble. The descent was at a much-too-steep angle.

At the last moment, with a roar of jets, it swerved and lifted its nose. It hit the widest part of the field in front of the assembly rooms, plowing up a huge furrow of dirt, waving it away in spatters, and shakily landing in an explosion of jet fire and rattles. It skidded along shakily like a puppet ship dangling on barely visible wires. Braking jets banged into action, but too late: the hopper smashed directly into the side of an outbuilding, splintering it in two.

Smoke twirled out.

The ship twitched, engines whining, shrilling. Then it came to a total, exhausted stop.

The driving rain doused the fires of its jets.

Jack smelled the burning exhaust.

No one was getting out of the thing.

They could only stare at the newly arrived vessel for a few heartbeats. It was Jack who brought the silence to an end.

"C'mon. The passengers may be hurt."

Quickly, they ran to the hopper. The glass of the passenger compartment was filmed over with condensation. Jack grabbed a hand and pulled. Locked. He knocked frantically on the windshield.

"Who's in there?" he demanded. "Are you okay?"

There were muffled voices from inside.

Something clicked, and hydraulics moved the doors up.

The coughing passengers made their way outside, helped by Took and Jane.

Jack recognized them immediately.

"Liz . . . Matt . . . My God, Orrin," he said. "What the hell are you doing here?"

"The kids . . . The kids," muttered Orrin, hand on his head, eyes glazed and dazed. "Are the kids okay?"

"Yeah," said Matt. "I'm okay."

"Me too," said Liz. "Just a little shaken up." She looked up and seeing Took, immediately hugged her. "Tookie, Tookie, I'm so glad to see you. Jane! Jack! This couldn't be better! Where's Dad?"

"We could have had a better landing," said Matt.

"Hey, I did my best," said Orrin. "In case you hadn't noticed, there's a storm going on."

"You did just fine, Orrin," said Jack. "But please . . . tell us why you're here."

"The assassin," blurted Liz. "He's here. He's after Dad. He's going to kill as many as possible."

"You've got to stop him," said Matt.

"Whoa, whoa, there," said Jane. "Slow down there. What are you talking about?"

"Your friend," said Orrin. "That man I saw you with, Jane. . . . That's him. He's the assassin who killed the Tarn businessman."

"What. You don't mean Ted, do you?" asked Jane.

"Yes," said Orrin. "Ted. Ted Bickford. It must be just an alias. We believe he's come here with an assignment to kill Lieutenant Brogan."

"We've got to stop him!" said Liz.

"Where is he? Where's Dad?" demanded Matt.

"Why Ted was just with us," said Took.

"He went off to—" She turned and walked off, cupping her hands by her mouth. "Ted. Ted, come back. We need to talk to you."

There was no response, save for the drone of the rain and the howl of the storm.

Jack, however, noticed that the inhabitants of the lodge were making their way out.

With surprising slowness.

Well, at least with the advent of this hopper, he might be able to explain away the presence of *all* of the outside interlopers. His Tarn and Creon brothers wouldn't realize that their antics had been filmed by Jane and company.

"Jane. Quickly. I'm going to tell them that you came on this hopper."

"Whatever. That's not important now," said Jane. "Ted!" she called out. "Ted!"

"Jane," said Took. "Check your bag. The gun."

Jack watched as Jane Castle quickly rummaged through her bag.

"It's gone!" she said.

"That's what I was afraid of," said Took.

"No. He can't be . . ." said Jane. "I . . . I can't believe."

"Hard to accept as it may be," said Orrin, "it's why we came all this way in the middle of a storm. Couldn't reach you by radio. Brogan's kids risked their necks—and mine—to get here to tell you that. It's a longer story than we have time to relate. I suggest that right now you just locate this fellow Ted Bickford. Stop him. His guilt or innocence we can determine later."

"That seems fine to me," said Jack. "But he's gone. Any idea of what's going on?"

Jane Castle looked stricken. "I'm not entirely sure, Jack. But I don't like the looks of it."

"I must say," said Took, "I have been suspicious of the man from the very start."

"Where *is* Dad?" demanded Liz.

"Yes. Where is the lieutenant?" said Orrin. "Seems that's the most important thing. Making sure he's safe now—and puttin' him in a place that will keep him safe."

"He's out with Captain Podly," said Haldane, brain-wheels spinning madly. "Hunting expedition."

"Hunting expedition?" said Matt. "In the middle of a storm?"

"Podly and Cradla—another bigwig—were dead set on it. I only just managed to wriggle my way out," said Jack. "I suppose one of the other hunting sorts can tell us which way they went." He turned to the approaching males. "In fact, here they come now."

However, as soon as he got a good look at his colleagues—Creon and Tarn alike—Jack Haldane knew that something was terribly wrong. They had been slow getting here, and now Jack could see why. They seemed to be *shambling* rather than walking. Their arms were loose and held out at odd angles. Their eyes looked dead and unseeing. Drool ran down the sides of their faces. And set in the mouths of those faces were things that Tarns and Creons simply weren't supposed to have.

Fangs.

"Hey, guys. What the hell is this?" said Jack nervously. "Halloween?"

Among their ranks, Jack distinguished the Creon named Xarday.

"*Koshva,*" said Xarday, as the group lunged forward with surprising speed, grabbing hold of the arms of the humans and Orrin and holding them fast in their places. "*Koshva!*"

Jack Haldane had the sudden feeling that this *koshva* stuff did not bode particularly well for them.

CHAPTER

As the storm stirred in the sky and beat its wet and wind upon the rocks, they made their way through the jagged rocks of the stone path, Cradla in the lead, Brogan and Podly behind. Podly began to speak after a time of quiet marching.

"You see, Lieutenant Brogan—no, excuse me, Patrick. You humans often prefer bein' called by your first names, and I'd like to honor your customs just as you've honored ours," said the Creon, in carefully thought-out phrasing. "Patrick. The hunting of the *zark* has come to have a very special meaning to the members of our organization. Would you like to hear why?"

"Of course he would, Podly," said Cradla brusquely. "Humans are remarkably inquisitive creatures."

"You're quite right, Cradla," said Brogan. "That we are." He turned to his captain. "Sir, it would mean a great deal to me if I knew why this *zark* hunting is so very important to your organization."

"Good. Because I'd very much like to tell the story of how it came to be. In fact, perhaps it would be best to tell you how this whole enterprise, this whole business of Dreek Island, came to exist."

"I'd enjoy that," said Brogan.

They stumped along in silence for a moment, their armor shifting and clanking slightly. Even the rain seemed to let up somewhat, as though pausing to hear the tale.

"Now, Brogan," said Podly, "I realize that you probably think that I have not been myself lately."

"Well, sir, humans are used to discovering differing facets of personality in people," said Brogan.

"I prefer consistency myself, particularly when it comes to performing one's duty. This is why I have come to respect you and your fellow Earthers—despite your own peculiar idiosyncrasies. Nevertheless, there come times even in the lives of Creons in authority when one must— well, I'm not sure what the term would be in human vernacular."

"Loosen up? Let down your hair?" suggested Brogan.

"Ah. Absolutely. Something along those lines, yes. This has been what has been happening here these past days, and I suspect you may be surprised by my behavior."

"Enthusiasm is always an attractive quality to

me, Captain. And you've been nothing less than enthusiastic about this whole business."

"Indeed, so I have. Now—to the explanation." Podly cleared his throat. "It is not an easy thing, this policing of Demeter City."

"You don't have to tell me that. I *do* it."

"Yes. However, long before your time here . . . Well, it was even more difficult. The place was total chaos. Who would have known that the city that the Creons and Tarns built as a coenterprise would be so near the byways of interstellar passage? The spaceport was barely open and we immediately attracted the wrong element. Tarns and Creons had allowed for a small police force, commensurate with the troubles expected from our own cultures. However, as soon as Demeter City expanded into a megalopolis, crime mushroomed. We were absolutely overcome! This is why we had to withdraw Precinct 88 from downtown Demeter City and place it in synchronous orbit. Naturally, there are other cities on Altor, other police forces who use this island. But they did not have the problems we did.

"Let me tell you, Brogan. The Demeter City Police Force at that time was a shattered outfit. The morale was at an all-time low. As though all this was not bad enough, Tarns and Creons were only used to cooperating in times of harmony. This terrible business of wholesale crime threatened to tear the whole force apart.

"Then, one of my predecessors, a Creon named Maxon, leader of the GOKS, had a brainstorm. He took a number of the best officers on the force—and at that time, the force was entirely male—to a retreat upon this very island. He invited the Tarns to join the GOKS. It was a masterstroke. These officers—hardly a team—were able to relax and form bonds of friendship and cooperation.

"The one problem with Dreek Island, however, was that it was overrun with vicious, nasty beasts known as *zarks*. This was an evolutionary aberration, and indeed was destroying the ecological balance of the island.

"A decision was made by Maxon. The *zark* population had to be reduced. However, rather than merely reduce them by killing them from safe positions or by other means, Maxon chose to see it as a challenge for individuals. He decreed that the *zark* population should be lowered by hunting them."

Brogan could hear Podly take a heavy breath within the armor. "This was not an easy decision. Maxon knew it would be risky. In fact, three police officers in the first two years of that initial push were killed by *zarks*—including Maxon's best friend. Even now, as you have learned, *zarks* make their claim upon the lives of our people.

"Only something in the execution of these hunting parties occurred. Away from the confusing artificiality of Demeter City and back in the deep dwellings of the instinct upon this island, Creons and Tarns formed deep bonds in these hunting parties. They learned to work together, cohere on a very basic level. Within days of the first week spent upon Dreek Island, the police force of

Demeter City began to come together as a single, functioning unit. We, at last, were a team.

"So you see, Brogan. This is why I am so 'enthusiastic' about Dreek Island. And why the hunting of the *zark* is so important to me. It not only allows rest and recreation—it is almost a symbolic ritual of the teamwork that brings different sorts together on a dangerous, grand, and very vital enterprise: lawkeeping on the most dangerous city in the galaxy. Demeter City."

"Aye," said Cradla. "And the *zark* gets to be the sacrifice."

Podly barked a laugh. "The *zark*, my friend, as you well know, can fend for itself." He gestured. "Besides, now, that the *zark* population is under control, Dreek Island is a model of ecology. All manner of flora and fauna thrive. True, many thrive upon one another, but that, after all, is Nature, is it not?"

"That it is," said Cradla. "But surely it is the role of one species to evolve and dominate."

"Dominate. I have heard that word so often from you, Cradla," said Podly. "It is not only misleading, it is inaccurate. Far better to use the word 'coordinate.' Yes, that is what we of the force do, is it not, Patrick? We do not dominate citizens. We coordinate them through the use of laws beneficial to the commonweal."

"Sounds noble enough," said Brogan. "Back in New York I guess we just all thought of it as a dirty job that someone had to do. I think I like your version much better, Captain Podly."

"Thank you. I appreciate that." He turned to their guide. "Cradla. Any indication of a *zark* nearby?"

Cradla paused. His head reared up pensively. There was a huge intake of breath.

Then he said, "Up a little farther, I think! Be prepared!"

"Excellent!" Podly lifted his gun, switching off the safety. "But surely, Patrick—perhaps you'd like to have the first shot."

"No, I think I'll just stand as backup."

"Good enough." Podly gestured as though he were a wagonmaster announcing a journey west. "Onward. Cradla has found us a *zark* and I mean to bring one back this evening."

They went on for a while. The path, after reaching the crest of a hill, turned downward and journeyed into a field of rocks and curious bent trees.

Brogan felt just as uncomfortable as before. However, with Podly's story, he had a better attitude about the whole undertaking. It was a shame that beings had to find unity in killing—but then, the Creons and the Tarns were just as close to the savage part of the evolutionary paths as were human beings. If that power for bonding existed, and the part of one's essential nature had to be tapped—well, so be it.

He certainly could relate.

After some minutes of quiet travel, Cradla stopped them.

"I smell it. There's one just up ahead. Be on your guard, gentle beings."

Brogan examined his own weapon, then gingerly pushed the safety bolt off.

He could feel adrenaline charge through his system and a taste of fear enter his mouth.

Slowly, cautiously, they progressed.

Then Cradla held up a hand. "Yes, indeed," he said. "Just up ahead and around that corner. It seems to be either sleeping or conveniently waiting for us. Podly—if you mean to make the initial attempt, perhaps you should go first."

"Initial attempt?" said Podly. "Initial nothing! I shall put it down on my own."

"Nonetheless, there is no telling if you'll be needing backup, now is there? That's why we're here," Cradla reminded him.

"True. Too true. Thanks for that. My eagerness gets the better of me." Podly struck out ahead.

Brogan waited for Cradla to continue.

"No, no," said the Creon. "I shall bring up the rear, I think. I sense the possibilities of other *zarks* roaming in these environs and I should be at a point where I can guard the rear."

That seemed to make a great deal of sense to Brogan. Although there was no reason why he should not stay on guard himself.

They progressed, cautiously.

Brogan could feel a trickle of sweat dripping down his forehead. He could smell his fear and exhilaration inside his suit. Time seemed to slow down. He felt completely aware and alive.

They made the turn, ducking under a low-hanging branch of a mossy, dripping tree.

"There!" said Cradla, voice tense and excited. "Just up ahead. Be careful."

At first Brogan saw nothing. Then, slowly, as his eyes adjusted, he began to make out the thing.

Upon a rising hill, among boulders and thatches of bent and scruffy little trees, was a swath of ragged fur with a flurry of stripes. The creature seemed camouflaged by the mottled brown and black of its surroundings.

But then it stirred and Brogan could indeed make it out.

First of all, it was big.

Much bigger than any of its Earthly feral equivalents, Brogan could see—the nearest equivalent would be one of the saber-toothed tigers that used to roam prehistoric Earth.

Only saber-tooths didn't have six legs. Six legs that were more like claw trees.

The *zark's* head seemed to be a thicket of fangs and barbs, through which blazing yellow eyes glared.

The thing snarled, and yet more barbs, like fish-hooks, unfurled along its spine.

Brogan whistled. "Nasty!"

"Moderate-sized," said Cradla.

"Aye," said Podly. "I've seen worse." He lowered his weapon. "A tough nut, though, with a lot of protection from the look of it. Cradla, Patrick. Perhaps you'd better back me up."

"Certainly," said Cradla.

Brogan could hear a ratcheting sound as Cradla prepared his power rifle. He lifted his own, adjusted the sights on the scaly thing snarling before him.

The thing seemed frozen in preternatural fury, and Brogan could almost feel it getting ready to spring.

"Concentration, Podly," said Cradla. "Concentration, please. Remember last time. You missed the first shot last time."

"Silence, Cradla. I'll not miss this time," said Podly.

The creature leaped. Podly tracked, fired. A bolt of energy shot out, glancing off one side. The thing roared with pain, and the impact of the power bolt pushed it off to the side and down the hill. It rolled, snapping and shrieking.

Something prickled at the back of Patrick Brogan's neck.

Some sixth sense made him turn.

Just in time to catch the butt of Cradla's swinging rifle.

CHAPTER

The large vat of liquid was just starting to boil.

Jane Castle could feel its heat as she sat close to it, her hands and feet bound. The others of her party were similarly tied.

Creons and Tarns alike danced around the flaming cauldron, a strange, smelly brew slopping from their mugs. Jane had seen this cauldron before and she didn't like the looks of it up close any more than she had liked it from beyond the window.

"Haldane," she said, "what's going on? They're not going to cook us and eat us, are they?"

"They don't exactly look in their right minds, do they?" said Haldane.

"They look absolutely drugged out of their minds!" said Matt Brogan.

"Bonkers," said Liz. "Totally bonkers."

"Hey, guys," said Orrin. "It's me, guys. Your buddy. What the hell are you trying to prove?"

"*Koshva*," they began to chant. "*Koshva!*" Their eyes were blank and vapid, Jane could see. They acted not at all like the police officers she knew and worked with, but rather like zombies. Programmed zombies.

But programmed for *what*?

"That's some kind of stuff that Xarday wanted to get ahold of," said Jack. "What the hell it does, I haven't the faintest."

"Looks to me as though it turns them into zombies," said Matt, echoing Jane's thoughts.

The police officers seemed to be participating in some kind of ritual involving the liquid in the vat.

Jane breathed a little bit easier. "Well, it would seem at least as though they're not going to cook us or anything."

"Just what are your intentions!" demanded Liz, struggling in her bonds.

"*Koshva*," said the police zombies. "*Koshva!*"

"Just like men," said Jane. "So repetitious."

"Dad's in danger. We've got to get out of here and warn him," said Matt.

"I'll take any suggestions on procedure!" said Jack.

Jane looked at Took. "Any tricks up your sleeve, Took?"

The Tarn nodded. "I'm working on it," she whispered. "These officers have indeed been drugged—and I'm beginning to suspect, by their states of mind, exactly what is happening."

"So—tell us," said Jane.

"No time. I need to concentrate. Just keep your hands very still, Jane. I learned this trick in the equivalent of your Earth's Girl Scouts."

Took's middle eye began to open.

Almost immediately, Jane felt a tug on her bonds. So that was what her friend was doing . . . Not only did she have powers of telekinesis—she knew her way around knots. That was something that most certainly these males would have no idea she was capable of doing. Especially not in the state they were in.

And what a state. They were bumbling and fumbling about, totally oblivious of anything but the liquid they were concocting. Whatever attention they had seemed totally devoted to the process, which was fine by Jane. Their inattention to their prisoners might just give Jane and her friends the opportunity they needed.

Jane could feel the ropes around her hands loosening. Within moments, her arms were free. No one was looking their way yet.

Swiftly, she untied her legs, then attended to the others. By the time she got round to Took, the able telekinetic had already freed herself.

Psychic powers certainly came in handy sometimes!

"Quickly. Jack—you know which way Brogan and Podly went?"

"Yes, I think so."

"Then we've got to go help Dad!" said Liz.

"Exactly. I think we'll be able to outrun our

erstwhile captors, but we'll have to make a start of it now."

Even as Jane spoke, a Creon drew forth a batch of the liquid and started to bring it their way. Clearly it was his intent that the prisoners should share this incapacitating liquid.

It was time to make their departure.

"That way," said Haldane, and they all ran.

CHAPTER

The end of the rifle whacked the side of Brogan's head.

It was insufficient to knock him out, but it was enough to knock him down and daze him.

He went down onto the sodden ground, hard. Although he was able to see the things that happened next, he was unable to do anything about them.

Cradla swung the rifle around, aiming the business end at Podly.

"Captain!" Brogan cried as best he could, attempting to fling himself at his captain's attacker.

Podly swung around, moving sufficiently to take the blast in the arm, not his body. The force of the blast pushed him down.

"Oh well," said Cradla. "Not quite as I'd planned, but I'll just have to make do."

He aimed directly at Podly and was about to pull the trigger when a "crack" sounded from the hill above. Something smacked directly into Cradla's armor, pushing him aside. A bullet! However, Cradla's armor was apparently well reinforced at the point of impact. The bullet did not penetrate.

With astonishing speed, Cradla swung around, looked up. In the same fluid motion the Creon brought his already-prepared rifle up, aimed, and fired.

The energy bolt whapped into something out of Brogan's range of vision. There was a grunt, a gasp, and a singed body tumbled onto the path. Smoke rose up from a gaping hole in the chest. Brogan smelled the awful stench of burned flesh.

It was a man who had fallen, and he was most certainly dead. Brogan did not recognize him. If he had had the luxury, he would have been confused.

Right now, though, he was struggling to claw his way from his dazed and stunned condition. He tried to get up, but was rewarded with another blow to the head from Cradla's boot, sending him reeling back into a prostrate position. Blurrily, he could see Podly crawling toward his own weapon. Cradla kicked the rifle away and then booted Podly in the head as well.

"It appears you had a human protector I did not know about," said Cradla, sneering down at the burned body. "Little good that it did you."

Brogan tried to say something but could not. It was all he could do to remain conscious. He held hard to his awareness with every fiber of his being.

Podly said, in a pained voice, "Cradla. I don't understand!"

"No, I shouldn't think you would, Podly. You're too busy running the city to see what's going on underneath your nose. Well, it's just about all done now. You'll be gone soon and I shall be the new captain. Only the police force will be quite, quite different than it was before."

"Envy? Jealousy? Is that it, Cradla?" said Podly. "All this time your wounds have festered because I was promoted above you?"

"I am a slave to classical emotions, Podly. Yes, yes, yes. Now, though, it makes little difference."

"Maelish! You killed Maelish, didn't you?"

"I did," said Cradla. "Nor will there be an inquest from the new Space Precinct, you see. For, unlike you, I shall have complete control of my officers—and it shall be the beginning of a thorough control, finally, of Demeter City." There was a pause, and Brogan could imagine a sly smile forming on that thick, ridged face. "Already here on Dreek Island the officers are becoming *mine.*"

"What are you talking about, Cradla?"

"I may as well tell you, Podly," said Cradla. "You won't live to see it and it will give me immense satisfaction knowing that you'll go to your death knowing the future that is in store for your precious police force. Drugs, Podly. Mind control. All the officers here on Dreek Island are falling under my power. In two days, their minds will be totally within my control."

"Cradla. This isn't you. What's happened?" said Podly.

"Happened, Podly? What has happened?" Cradla raised his rifle, adjusted the power supply. "There are neither words nor time enough, Podly. First I shall dispose of you, then this meddling human here." Cradla turned to Brogan. "Lieutenant, I just wanted you around long enough to know that all your efforts to bring your accursed Earth ways to Demeter City will be for naught. One of my first chores in my new capacity will be to eradicate human beings from Demeter City and send your silly race packing back to the isolated planet where it belongs."

"You're—a—swell—guy, Cradla," Brogan managed.

"Thank you. It's nice to be appreciated. Now both of you, please kiss existence good-bye."

Cradla was raising the rifle and in the act of pointing it at Podly, when the most remarkable thing happened.

The chest of the dead man popped open, spraying an odd combination of flesh, blood, and circuitry.

From this chest rose up a two-foot-tall humanoid, draped with wires. In his hands was a gun.

"I don't think so, Cradla."

A spurt of fire emerged from the gun, flashing and crashing into Cradla's weapon. The rifle exploded, pushing the Creon back against the rock face of the cliff.

Cradla reached for a sidearm.

However, something had freed up in Brogan's motor control. He used his increased capacities immediately, leaping forward and plowing a shoulder into the Creon.

Cradla's grip on the hand weapon was lost and it clattered to the ground. Brogan banged his helmet against the rock so hard that it came off.

Somehow, though, Cradla broke free. He staggered back, looking disoriented. Then he made to run back to obtain his weapon.

"Oh no you don't!" said Podly. The police captain extended a leg and tripped his rival. Cradla went down with a clatter of his armor. He rolled and pushed himself up, scraping along to get hold of the gun that would give him the upper hand.

Brogan stepped forward and kicked the gun farther away.

With an astonishing show of strength, Podly pushed himself to his feet, grabbed Cradla by the arm, and spun him around.

"Internal Affairs speaking, Cradla."

Podly punched him directly in the face.

The stricken Cradla windmilled backward. The back of his sturdy boot caught the edge of a rock and he toppled over the edge, rolling down into a wealth of brush with considerable yelping. He crashed through the branches and was swallowed up by the flora.

Almost immediately, there was the roar of a *zark*.

"Podly! Help. Pod—"

Cradla's cry was cut off by a sharp tearing sound.

The bushes shook violently, accompanied by a great deal of snarling and snapping.

So much for Cradla apparently, thought Brogan. And fortunately the wounded *zark* now had something to occupy himself with while he and Podly gathered their wits.

But who was this thing that had popped out of the dead human and what was he doing here.

He swung around to have a look.

"Hello, Patrick Brogan," said the alien being, jewellike eyes glittering as he extended a hand in greeting. "I am very happy to have made it here in time."

"Who the hell are you?" asked Podly.

The creature bounced out of the android carcass. "A very good question and I'm quite glad you asked."

However, the alien creature was interrupted by desperate shouts.

CHAPTER

The rain had lessened
somewhat and the shriek of the winds had stilled
when Jane Castle heard the rifle blasts.

"Over there!" cried Jack Haldane.

"No kidding," said Jane, who was already running along the stony path in the direction of the
sounds.

The others in the party were not far behind:
Took, Liz and Matt Brogan, and Orrin, all making
the best they could of the hard going among the
rocks.

They were all tired from the search, but under
Jack's guidance, they'd found evidence of the hunting party's progress and direction. It had been
Took's psychic ability that had guided them up this
way, and now their efforts were about to pay off.

Jane hoped.

However, when she finally made the turn after a couple of minutes of hard-breathed running, she ran into a scene that astonished and horrified her:

Here were Podly and Patrick Brogan (thank heavens they were safe!) in a battered state, confronting some sort of alien creature with glittery, jewellike eyes. It was humanoid, but it had crests on its back and a huge ridged forehead. Gossamer webs stretched across numerous digits on its flat, winglike hands. It was standing amid a pile of limbs and a torso that looked . . . well, human and . . .

Jane gasped as she moved closer.

"Oh my God!"

She recognized the face attached to the androidal corpse.

Ted Bickford!

"Ted!"

The jewel-eyed being turned toward her. "Oh. Hello, Jane. Sorry to give you such a start."

She found her mouth moving, but nothing came out.

"Jane Castle," said Podly. "What are you doing here?"

Brogan didn't seem quite so astonished to see her. "You know this character, Jane? He just more or less saved our bacon."

"Where's Cradla?" asked Jack.

"*Zark* food," said Podly. "Just as well. Apparently he had some grandiose plan for Demeter City that involved taking over Precinct 88."

"Tell me about it," said Jack. "He's already got a

band of raving and drooling zombies back there who were trying to force us to guzzle some sort of drug."

"That would be *koshva*," said Jewel-Eyes.

"Your friend seems to know a lot," said Brogan. "He was about to tell us a story. Care to pull up a chair?"

"I think, Brogan, you'd better deal with a little greeting first," said Jane, still stunned as she stared at what was left of Ted . . . or rather, what he had become.

Intimate memories flooded into her head, startling her.

"Dad!"

"Dad, you're okay!"

The Brogan kids swept past her.

Patrick Brogan was clearly astonished to see them. They ran into his arms, hugging him.

"An assassin—he might be trying to kill you," said Liz.

"We found out and we came to warn you and—" Matt looked down at the previous body of the jewel-eyed alien and pointed. "That's *him*!"

Orrin, newly arrived, heard this and stepped over to have a look. "Yes, it is indeed." He pulled his gun, trained it on the newly emerged alien. "I suggest you try nothing violent, guy."

"The furthest thought from my mind at this point," said Jewel-Eyes. "But allow me to introduce myself. My name is Gothan-Zox of the Galactic Secret Investigations Unit—"

"What?" said Podly.

"Please. I was about to get around to an explanation. We are a supraplanetary law enforcement agency," said Gothan-Zox. "We monitor the things normal policy agencies cannot know, and tweak this and that to maintain the cosmic equilibrium, so to speak."

"You don't deny that you're an assassin, that you killed that Tarn businessman," said Podly.

The little alien brushed a bit of circuitry from his previous habitation off his shoulder and stepped out of "Ted Bickford." "True, that was the personality and skill overlay I was wearing that did that. Our ways are not your ways. Zin Mooka was involved in the same conspiracy that Cradla was a part of—a plan to take over the police force of the city."

"You could have notified us," said Podly. "You could have let us deal with it in our own way."

"No, Podly." Those strange eyes seemed to glitter with a mysterious depth. "Even now your men are wrapped up in drugs and mind control. It will take time for it to wear off. But think—you too have been involved with this mind control—and are a victim of it."

"What the hell are you talking about?"

"I am only at liberty to give a name—and perhaps it is a false one—to my organization," said the alien. "Perhaps I am not truly who I say I am. I remain enigmatic because that is the nature of my work, and in this sort of atmosphere we do what we do best." He looked over to Brogan. "Indeed, we even have agents on your planet . . ." A smile. "In fact, I was one myself. But I digress. Podly—you are a victim, as I said, of another kind of mind control. And an insidious one it is."

"I think perfectly well, thank you!" said Podly. "And I do it all by myself, with no outside control."

"You delude yourself. You are a victim of tradition and wrong thinking. A glaring example is the inequality on your force. Why is it that no females are allowed to come here?"

"It's . . . It's just not done!"

"True, it's clearly a bonding experience for the males that was of some importance when the force was entirely made up of such. But times have changed. Some of the most important members of your unit are female. Two stand here with me now. You may think it a small thing, but inequality is never small. It feeds dissension and unrest and creates much hatred and dissatisfaction. You need merely look at the history of Earth to see the damage done by class systems, nationalism—slavery. The list goes on. No, Podly. You are a victim of a mind control as well. And was this Cradla not also? He felt brushed aside by the system, and that started the evil in him. If he had merely been happy with the job he had, there could have been no corruption.

"A universal truth, encountered throughout the Universe. Big things always start out as small things. It is only when they are small that they can be dealt with. When they reach larger proportions, they are simply unmanageable." He paced and put up a finger. "This, indeed, is the purpose for our organization. We try to keep things manageable by dealing with them when they are small. Our methodologies are occasionally severe, true. But I ask you—how many good people would have died if that Tarn businessman continued—if Cradla continued. Someone has to nip the thorns in the bud!"

"That," said Brogan, "is still unconscionable. I'm afraid we're going to have to put you under arrest."

"I'm afraid he's right, Ted. We appreciate your help here, but you broke the law," said Jane.

The little alien seemed aghast.

"What—but I saved your lives!"

"That will most certainly be taken into account at the trial," said Podly. "Sorry, fellow. And it's not because of what you said about my mind control. I'm beginning to see the truth in your words. No, Brogan is right. You broke a law on Demeter City. You're under arrest."

The little alien squared his shoulders. "Very well. I'll come along peaceably. I've done my duty as I see it. You can't fault me for that. But you'll also get nothing more out of me as to my organization."

"I don't think we expected to," said Jane Castle. "Nor can we particularly believe it." She shook her head. "I can't believe you deceived me so. . . . Those years ago. I was . . . misled, wasn't I?"

The alien sighed. "Jane, Jane. Just because I'm not human doesn't mean I don't have feelings—I don't care. You speak of the need for equality, for lack of discrimination. Look in your own heart. I think you'll find enough prejudice to keep you plenty busy for a while."

"We'd better go back and deal with some drugged-out zombies," said Haldane.

"As a matter of fact, may I suggest an antidote that should work quite well?" said Gothan-Zox. "It would seem as though I still must rack up good deeds to compensate for my crime on Demeter City."

"All will certainly be mentioned at the trial," said Brogan.

"Good. Then you will have it. All's well that ends well, it would seem—except for poor little me."

The eyes glittered mischievously as the party headed back for the compound to deal with the troubles there.

"You don't want to take your body along?" said Jane.

"No," said Gothan-Zox. "Quite ruined. It served its purpose quite well, thank you."

Jane Castle took one look at the thing, a dead machine in the rain, and shuddered.

EPILOGUE

"I can't believe that you two managed to get all way out to Dreek Island," said Patrick Brogan in what served as the Space Precinct's conference room.

"Neither can I," said Sally Brogan, frowning at her children. She had been summoned as soon as they'd returned and was relieved to find them safe. She'd already put in a call about their disappearance.

"We couldn't have done it without Officer Orrin!" said Liz, patting the Creon on the lower back.

"Yeah. I could maybe have driven that hopper . . ." said Matt. "But not through that storm!"

"You're not old enough to drive anything yet," admonished their mother. "And when you are, I've a mind to ground you the moment you get your license!"

"Sally, they were convinced they were out to save my life—or the life of some other police officer," said Brogan. He, too, was upset with his kids, but he couldn't fault their motives. Also, they'd been wise enough to bring along an adult professional. If indeed that was what you cared to call Orrin.

"Damned fine kids, if you ask me," boomed Podly. "You in particular, Liz. Finding that Tarn object."

"I don't know where it came from or why it was in that park," said Liz.

"Simple," Brogan said, "I found it at the scene of the crime and was trying to puzzle it out. It and the bag it was in must have popped out of my pocket while we were playing ball or Frisbee. That thing had a strange effect on me. I'm not really sure why I took it with me on the picnic."

"Maybe Zin Mooka, the Tarn businessman, knew he'd seen his own killer and *willed* the jewel to eject," suggested Matt.

"Yes, and his soul sent us to help!" added Liz.

"That hardly ever happens," said Took thoughtfully. "But perhaps that is the case here."

"All the pieces come together—" said Haldane. "They make an odd weave, true. But at least they come together."

"I wonder who left us that note, though, that cautioned us to beware," said Brogan.

"Guess we'll have to wait to find that out. Nice to know we had another friend on the island, though. Could have saved us in ways we weren't even aware of," said Haldane. "Anyway, all's well that ends well."

Too, too correct, thought Brogan.

They'd come back to the encampment to find it truly a mess, with the officers a confused mass of straggling brainless wonders. Cradla must have had them primed for hypnotic commands from him alone. Without him, they were brainless automatons, drooling and stumbling. The other returning segment of the hunting party, unaffected by the *koshva,* once an explanation had been given them of Cradla's nefarious activities, eagerly aided them in herding the affected male officers together. With Gothan-Zox's help in concocting an antidote, the Creons and Tarns were put right—albeit with severe hangovers.

They slept through the storm.

The next morning, the sun was out upon Dreek Island.

Brogan had never known a more pleasant day upon the planet Altor. Everything seemed at peace.

He was merely happy to be alive.

Now, though, he was simply happy to be back once more with all his family.

"Not quite *everything* is well," demurred Jane Castle. "There's a little matter of inequality among the corps."

Podly waved his hand. "Yes, right. That matter. Well, I should tell you that I've had some very serious thoughts on the subject." His face was stern. Brogan was half-expecting a stormy argument on the subject. "After the events on Dreek Island, and your formal complaint—" He rippled a piece of paper in his hand. "Very well written, I might add. . . . And well reasoned, Officer Castle. I suppose you could say that I have 'seen the light' so to speak. I am calling a special meeting of the police commissioners to address this matter—and would like you to attend the meeting to present your point of view."

The room seemed to brighten with Jane's smile. "Thank you, Captain Podly. This makes me think I should have come to you first instead of trying to gather evidence."

Podly gave a wry half grin. "What? With my thick head. Never would have worked. Besides, you would never have brought that alien along to save my hide." The captain looked over to Brogan. "Speaking of which, weren't you and Haldane going to have a little Q and A with the fellow today?"

"Just on our way for that interrogation," said Haldane. "Jane, would you care to come with us?" Haldane managed admirably to refrain from smirking.

"No. I've nothing to say to him," said Jane, damping down the smile. "And I don't care to hear anything *he* has to say."

Brogan shrugged. He could well understand. It must be tough knowing that the last good romance you had wasn't even with a human. Of course, sometimes that seemed to be the way that a lot of women on Earth felt.

Sometimes, alas, even Sally.

"Okay, then," said Brogan. "If you'll excuse us." He gave Sally a kiss on the forehead and winked at his kids. "See you at dinner."

"You'll tell us what you can about that guy?" said Matt.

"Yeah, Dad. We'd really like to know."

"Of course. Once I clear it with Captain Podly," said Brogan. "Come on, Jack. Let's go down and see what we can find out."

The cell was empty, but for one item.

The bed was neatly made, except for a folded note.

"He's gone!" said Haldane.

"Brilliant observation, Sherlock," said Brogan. He raced out and hit the alarm.

The entire ship was searched.

Neither hide nor hair nor any alien analogues were discovered.

Gothan-Zox had seemingly vanished into thin ether.

When this baffling conclusion had been reached, Brogan remembered the note and opened it.

It read:

Sorry not to stick around for the formal proceedings, but you can't blame me really, can you?

My work is done and I must be on my way.

Perhaps we shall meet another day, when

law does not come between us and mere truth
and common sense rule.

—Gothan-Zox

They showed the note to Podly, who merely
grunted. The captain seemed neither to be too surprised nor chagrined at the whole business. "Well,
saves us the court costs, anyway. Besides, what
would we have done with him?"

"Treated him equally," said Jane Castle. "Just as
we would have treated any other citizen of the galaxy.
Justice, they say, is blind. And that's our job, isn't it?
Serving a blind being to the best of our ability."

"Hell," said Haldane. "I'm just trying to get
through this thing in one piece."

Jane looked at him. "You know, Jack. You may
be full of your self sometimes, but sometimes you
speak the total truth. Let's take our whole selves
and go play some gravball, eh? I feel the need to
sweat a little bit."

Jack agreed heartily, and they left for the gym.

Brogan was taking the letter from the alien
down for lab analysis when he noticed that somehow another line had magically appeared.

He stopped and read it.

P.S. Lieutenant Brogan. You have the mak-
ings of an excellent special agent. Perhaps
you'll be hearing from us one day.

Brogan shuddered. He certainly hoped not.
The Universe was strange enough as it was.

Canceling his thought about destroying the note with its addendum, he hurried onward to the lab, moving past a window with a view of the stars that seemed to peer into the station house— and Brogan's heart—with prying, never-ending curiosity.

CALIBAN'S HOUR by Tad Williams

Can an eternity of love be contained in an hour? The answer lies in the enchanting tale of magic and mystery from the *New York Times* bestselling author of *To Green Angel Tower* and *Tailchaser's Song*. ($4.99 Paperback)

DEMON SWORD by Ken Hood

An exhilarating heroic fantasy, *Demon Sword* takes place in the Scottish lands of a fanciful Renaissance Europe where our hero, an aspiring prizefighter named Toby, finds himself possessed by a demon spirit. But soon it appears that the king is possessed by the demon spirit and Toby is possessed by the spirit of the king! ($4.99 Paperback)